WITCHNAPPED IN WESTERHAM

Paranormal Investigation Bureau #1

DIONNE LISTER

Dionne Lister

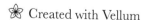 Created with Vellum

CHAPTER 1

The bride's nasally whine cut through the string quartet's soft music. "Hey, photographer, not there. Move that way a bit." She waved a large knife, indicating where I should go, the glossy white ribbon tied around the handle rippling with her efforts. "Remind me again why I'm paying you when I'm giving all the direction?"

God help me, but I wanted to shove her face into the wedding cake. Deep breaths. I tried to smile while I took a step to the left. I looked through the viewfinder of my Nikon and assessed the shot. The whitewashed weatherboard walls and iron chandelier holding candles created a magical backdrop. So pretty.

"No! Oh my God, do I have to do everything myself?" she shrieked, and I started. The bride bore down on me, knife still in hand, and pushed my shoulder until I was situated exactly where she wanted.

Who said weddings were an easy way to earn money? The bride retreated to her spot next to the groom. At least he had the good grace to blush. I wondered if he was reassessing his choice of a life partner. Bad luck, buddy; you already put a ring on it. "Are we ready to cut the cake now?" she asked, heavily pencilled eyebrow raised, as if I'd been the one holding things up. Sheesh.

"Look this way," I said, my eye twitching. The bride, Tracy, rolled her eyes. I guess I was stating the obvious, but her husband had been looking at her, so what was I supposed to do? They both turned to the camera, Tracy's scowl quickly switching to a glowing smile. I snapped a few shots while they poised the tip of the knife on the icing then pushed the blade into the four-tiered work of art.

With Tracy occupied, I quickly stepped back to my original position and clicked away as they fed each other cake. Why hire me if you're not going to trust my judgement? It wasn't like I was the cheapest photographer out there, and I doubted Tracy had a degree in visual arts. Who'd come up with the "the customer is always right" saying? Honestly, most of the time, the customer had no idea about shot composition and lighting. A headache threatened as I thought about the editing suggestions that would be coming my way next week.

Her parents joined her, and her father leaned in for a hug. I quickly moved forward, focused the lens and clicked some close-ups. That would be an amazing shot—the emotion in his face brought tears to my eyes. I couldn't wait to see it on my large desktop screen. Except...

I blinked and stopped clicking. I must be tired, because her father seemed see through, like I imagined a ghost would be. I could see Tracy's mother through him. What the hell? I lowered the camera. And, of course, he was solid, normal again. *I must need more coffee.* Maybe Tracy's whole crazy-bride thing had me so stressed that I was hallucinating.

Feedback exploded from the speaker system, destroying my hearing with laser precision. A giggle followed, and then a woman's voice slurred out of the speakers. "Oopsie. Time to dance! Get your arses on the floor, peeps!" Taylor Swift blasted over the partygoers. So that was it for any conversation. I pulled my phone out of my back pocket and checked the screen. 8:45 p.m.: forty-five torturous minutes to go. At least the bride would be too busy to harass me, as her bridesmaids had dragged her onto the dance floor.

I slipped my phone back into my pocket and hoisted my camera in front of my face. This was probably one of my favourite parts of a wedding—the candid shots where everyone was having fun. Someone tapped me on the shoulder. I turned.

The bride's father stood there, solid as ever, thank God. He even smiled. "Hi, Lily. I wanted to say thank you very much for today. You helped make this an incredible day for my daughter. I know she can get a little carried away sometimes." He shrugged, as if to say "what are you gonna do?" Hmm, I could think of a few things. "Anyway, here's an extra something to show our appreciation." His smile was genuine when he handed me a white envelope. It all felt a bit Mafia.

"Um, thank you, Mr Papadakis. That's very kind of you." He had already paid me the full amount for the job via direct debit, but I could only assume this was extra cash. I really wanted to know how much, but I wasn't sure if it was polite to open the envelope in front of him.

"It's my pleasure. My wife and I can't wait to see all the pictures. Thanks again." He smiled and made his way to the dance floor to bust some moves with his daughter. What a nice dad.

I took a deep breath and fought an unexpected tear. If I ever got married, I didn't have a dad to celebrate with, or a mum. They disappeared when I was fourteen, presumed dead. Maybe I would just avoid the whole "getting married" thing, then I wouldn't have to worry about missing them being there. At least I still had my older brother, James. After my parents disappeared, he took care of me. Then later, he met and married a London girl. They lived just outside London, but he called me every week, and I knew I'd be getting a call later for my birthday. He'd been over there for six years, but he never forgot the important dates.

I nabbed the last of the shots for the night, said goodbye to the bride and groom without too much drama, then lugged my equipment to my Subaru and packed it into the back seat. Once behind the wheel, I locked the doors—one could never be too careful—and opened the envelope. I simulated a drum roll by vibrating my tongue on the roof of my mouth—okay, it didn't sound anything like a drum roll, but it was better than nothing. My ears rang from the loud music, but the crinkle of the envelope opening was still loud in the quiet car. I held my breath as I pulled out the contents... green plastic notes, which meant, oh my God! One thousand Aussie dollars in hundreds.

"Woohoo!" I screamed. This called for a song. "Happy birthday to me. Happy birthday to me. Happy birthday, dear Lily. Happy birthday to me!" Best present ever. One-thousand un-taxable dollars. I grinned. Maybe I could duck over to the UK sooner than I thought. This money was so going into my holiday/visit-my-brother fund. I turned the radio on and sung along with the latest pop tunes all the way home. Maybe turning twenty-four wasn't so bad after all.

Except, I may have spoken too soon.

CHAPTER 2

I walked in my door at 10.45 p.m., and I was ready to go to sleep, but I didn't want to miss James's call. There was a hot shower with my name on it, after which I replied to a couple of texts from my friends wishing me happy birthday and begging me to come out with them, but I wasn't in the mood. My birthday brought out the worst in me. I was normally a happy person, but depression came calling every birthday. It was easy to feel sorry for myself when I had no family to celebrate with. I missed the unconditional love I'd had when I was a kid—my parents' and grandparents' faces would light up when they saw me. The meals we'd have as a family, usually finished off with my grandmother's apple strudel, were always a delicious feast with much arguing and laughter.

Comfy in my jammies, I settled onto my fawn-coloured

couch and flicked through the channels. Yay that *Bridesmaids* was on, but boohoo that it only had twenty minutes left. It was my favourite comedy movie of all time. Maybe the universe was trying to make it up to me. I lay back on the couch, clutching my phone. At the end of the movie, I checked the iPhone screen. Nope, no calls, which I already knew, because the phone hadn't rung, but I had to be sure, like sure, sure.

I yawned. 11.30 p.m., which made it 2.30 p.m. over in England. He should've called by now, unless he got caught up at work. Maybe there'd been a coding emergency, and all his company's websites were down. That was more likely than him having forgotten, wasn't it? Although, we all forget things sometimes. Disappointment settled over me. Tears burnt my overreacting eyes. *Dammit, Lily, he'll call. Stop being such a baby.* I sniffled and wiped the heel of my hand over my eyes. *No more crying.*

Some other show called *Dating Naked* came on, where the contestants go on dates, you guessed it, naked. Oh, the horror of seeing people horse riding naked. Ew. I wouldn't want to be the person cleaning that saddle afterwards. And I had no idea about anyone else, but the last thing I wanted to see on a first date was the guy's junk, and trust me, I wasn't a prude; it just wasn't the most attractive part of a man. I was more of an "eyes and face" girl. Ah, late-night television, how you mock me. But I watched it, because it was better than staring at my phone. Okay, it wasn't really, but whatever.

Shortly after 1:00 a.m., and two god-awful episodes of *Dating Naked* later, I fell asleep, clutching my silent phone.

Argh, morning. I turned my face away from the gross damp spot on my favourite cushion and wiped dribble off my face. There was nothing like waking up on the couch with an emotional hangover. I squinted and could just make out the time on my phone. No missed calls. No messages. It was too early for more disappointment. Time for coffee. Until my first coffee of the morning, I was only capable of grunts, but when James called, I'd have to do words.

I turned the machine on and filled the thingamajig—I had no idea what it was called, but that lack of knowledge didn't affect my operating skills—with coffee grounds before screwing it into the main part of the machine. I pressed another button, but instead of hot water cascading through the grounds, sparks showered from the back of the machine.

"No!" I leaned over and ripped the plug from the wall, coughing through the smoke.

My coffee maker was dead. And what the hell? It was only twelve months old. I'd have to get the backup out—my stovetop percolator my grandmother left me when she died.

As I reached into the cupboard, my phone rang. It rang! Hmm, I didn't recognise the number. Maybe James had trouble with his phone and had to borrow someone else's?

"Hello?"

"Hello... Lily?" A woman's voice broke through the static, and it sounded like Millicent.

"Hello, Millicent?"

"Lily, hello? Are you there? It's—"

9

The line went dead. That was two deaths already this morning. Yes, they were metaphorical deaths, but the hairs on the back of my neck stood on end anyway, and I shuddered. Today was not looking good. Maybe I should've just gone back to bed.

However, I wasn't a giver-uperrer, so I pressed redial. It rang, but as soon as someone answered, the line cut out. Hmm. The reception in my apartment was always fine, but I moved to the window anyway.

I pressed redial. This time, it didn't even ring. I blew a raspberry, frustration lacing each droplet of spittle that flew from my tongue. Okay, then. Time to get dressed. I was failing at life this morning, so I'd let someone else make my coffee. The café down the street made a decent brew. Maybe I'd take a walk along the beach after I grabbed my coffee. That sounded like a plan.

I found black sports tights and a red T-shirt in my clean-clothes basket—I hated putting clothes away; it was so time-consuming and boring—and put them on. I dragged my sneakers out from under the bed and put them on too, grabbed my wallet, keys, and phone, and opened the door… to a slim, fifty-something-year-old woman in a grey suit, her hand poised to knock. Huh?

"Can I help you?" I couldn't see any brochures, so I was probably pretty safe from a religious lecture—not that I hated religion; I was agnostic, and I believed in my right to live peacefully in un-annoyed bliss with my choice, just as I believed others had a right to their beliefs without me judging them and demanding they all become fence-sitters, like me.

Her stern gaze raked me from head to toe and back again. Was my appearance the cause of her frown—my T-shirt *was* a little creased—or was it her super-tight bun? Actually, I didn't really want to find out.

"Look, I'm just on my way out, Ms…?"

"Angelica Constance DuPree, but Ma'am to you." *Okaaay.* As well as being bossy, she had a refined English accent, which gave her words more gravity. She tipped her head back so her nose pointed higher: all the better to look down at me. "And you're Lily Katerina Bianchi. You're about what I expected."

What was that supposed to mean? I blinked. My brain had nothing. Coffee. I needed coffee. Also, how did she know my name? I supposed she could have found it on the Internet. Was she a stalker? She could have a knife or some-thing tucked into the back of her skirt under her suit jacket.

"…Ma'am, would you like to chat while we walk? I have to get… somewhere." Coffee didn't sound important enough a reason to rush outside, but believe me, it was almost life and death. I'd have a migraine by lunchtime if I missed my daily caffeine hit. I eased past her and shut my door, the deadbolt automatically locking in place. It would probably be safer to talk to her in public. She gave off a cranky and slightly scary vibe, to be honest, oh, and she knew my name; let's not forget that.

"Very well, then. Once you get your coffee, we can come

back here and talk. This is a matter to be discussed in private."

Say again? How did she know I was going out for coffee? Did I look like a coffee junkie in withdrawals? Nah, someone suffering coffee withdrawals didn't look like anything, at least not until I opened my car door, leaned out and threw up from a migraine. Yes, it had happened. More than once. Don't judge me; Ma'am's judgey glares were all I could take right now. Ooh, she was also looking smug, like she had one over on me. I suppose being able to mind-read would make you feel like that. I wanted to read minds, dammit! I didn't really believe she could do that, did I?

Gah, I wanted coffee, like really, really badly, but this was crazy. I didn't know this woman. I was not letting her tag along, but how to say it? I wasn't usually one to speak my mind and be "difficult." Which was probably what got most women into situations they wished they'd avoided. Maybe it was time to learn to annoy people and not worry.

"Look, Ma'am, I don't know you, and I have no idea why you're at my front door, or how you know my name. I suggest you tell me what you want now, and get it over with. Frankly, I don't have the energy for weirdness today."

She narrowed her eyes, probably assessing my likelihood of running before she could stab me. I edged towards the stairs, ready to sprint one floor down to freedom.

Ma'am rolled her eyes and sighed. "Honestly, Lily, what are we going to do with you? I'm not here to hurt you; I'm here to protect and guide you."

And that didn't sound freaking weird at all. Stuff it. I

took off, bounding down the stairs two at a time until I was out the door, on the footpath, in public. Safe.

The sun shone on a cool morning, and it looked like the day was going to be gorgeous—weather wise, at least. It may have been rude of me to just leave like that, but I preferred to be safe now rather than dead. And that's not an overreaction. *Trust your gut* was one of those sayings I lived by. If I was wrong about Ma'am, I could always apologise later, and we'd laugh about it. Yep, or she wouldn't laugh and hold it against me forever.

I hurried along the footpath, past an assortment of unit blocks, from red-brick two-storey ones to rendered brick twelve-storey ones. Monday morning brought out a mixture of joggers, surfers, and people dressed for work. I crossed at the traffic lights and soon reached Surfer's Brew. The delectable fragrance of fresh coffee swirled around me. I breathed it in and sighed. Ah. That was more like it.

Just before entering, I looked back. No sign of my weirdo morning visitor. Maybe my morning was improving. I smiled and stepped up to the counter. "Morning, Frances. Can I get a regular skim cap?" I didn't get coffee here every day—because I had my coffee machine, or used to have— how depressing—but I visited regularly enough that they knew me. Sometimes I wanted something frothy with chocolate on the top, and I was too lazy to do that at home.

Frances was in her mid-thirties, had gorgeous straight blonde hair, which was pulled back in a sleek ponytail, and an infectious smile. "Hey, chicky. Coming right up. A little birdie told me it was your birthday yesterday. Happy birthday!" She banged used coffee grounds out of the thinga-majig and filled it with new ones.

"Aw, thanks. Did you run into the girls last night?" The girls being my besties, Sophie and Michelle.

"Yep. How come you weren't there? They told me you piked." She screwed the thingamajig into the machine and pressed the button. And wouldn't you know, it worked. I wish my machine still worked.

"Big day photographing a wedding. One drink and I would have fallen asleep." I laughed—it wasn't too far from the truth. So what if I left out the bit where I had a pity party because my brother hadn't called. I'd try calling him later. Knowing him, he had a good reason for missing my birthday, and I would keep reminding myself until I knew for sure.

Frances frothed the milk and poured it into the coffee before sprinkling lots of chocolate on the top—she did extra for me, because it was my favourite part. Then she did some magic with a spoon and made a cute little heart on the top of the froth. "There you go." She smiled, and I handed her four dollars—coffee habits didn't come cheap.

"Thanks. You're a lifesaver. See you later." I waved. She waved. The usual. I stopped just outside the shop, unpopped the lid and licked the chocolatey goodness off it before taking a sip. Heaven. The simple things were really the best.

I replaced the lid and started down the street, contem-plating whether I should return to my apartment, and possibly run into Ma'am, or go for that walk. There was nothing like a stroll on the beach to settle my mind. The rolling surf was calming. During summer, I'd go body surfing, but the water was a bit cool now, and I was the first to admit, I was soft.

Hmm, if I went back now and had to deal with Ms Crazy-pants, I wouldn't be able to enjoy my coffee properly. That was an easy decision: walk it was!

But since when was life that easy?

I reached the end of the path and the beginning of the sand. Salty sea spray hazed the air, seagulls wheeled overhead, and the sun warmed my face. Surfers bobbed in the water, waiting for the next wave, and a young mother watched her two kids build a sandcastle. Before I could absorb the peace of the scene, I noticed something, or rather someone, that was out of place: a woman in a drab but well-tailored business suit and low heels with her arms crossed in front of her chest and another self-satisfied smile. Seemed like she only had two expressions: pissed off and smug. I breathed in deeply, and when I exhaled, my serenity went with it. Wasn't it supposed to work the other way around?

"You can run, but you can't hide." Great, she was intimidating me with clichés.

"On a scale of one to ten, your creep factor is about an eight. Think you could tone it down?"

She smiled. It could have even been genuine this time. "At least you have some spunk. You're going to need it, missy." Her expression morphed into sad then quickly into serious.

I sipped my coffee. I had a feeling I was going to need all

the caffeine support I could get before she was done with me.

Angelica nodded. "Unfortunately, you're right."

Not again with the mind reading. How was she doing that? "Can you please tell me what you want?"

"Look, we don't have time to dilly-dally. You appear strong enough, at least, and there's no way to say this nicely, so I'll just say it. Your brother, James, is missing. He disappeared seven days ago."

No amount of coffee could have prepared me for that. My stomach fell as fast as my cup. It hit the ground, still half full, dammit. The lid came off, splashing brown liquid on my runners and shins. A chill sluiced the sun's warmth from my arms like the reaper's scythe, leaving goosebumps in its wake. I shivered.

I was transported back to the day my mum's best friend sat James and me down and explained that our parents weren't coming home. Ever again. I remembered James gripping my hand and squeezing for dear life. We'd held fast to each other since then, until he'd gone off to the UK. Tears spilled down my cheeks. I wanted to fall to the ground and curl into a ball, but making a scene wasn't going to help. Was James's disappearance somehow related to my parents'? Was I next? *No, don't be stupid, Lily. Coincidences exist. That's all it is.*

Ma'am stepped closer and laid a stiff hand on my shoulder. She patted me awkwardly then dropped her hand. I appreciated the gesture: I wasn't much of a hugger either.

My personal space was just as important to me as my right to believe in nothing.

"You look a little pale, dear. I'm sure you have many questions. Let's return to your apartment and grab your things. We have a plane to catch."

What? "Where to?"

"Why, London of course. Then we're driving to Westerham. You're going to help us find your brother. Hopefully he's still alive."

Hopefully? Nausea clutched my throat and squeezed. There was nothing I could do. Nothing. And who was "us"? Common sense wormed its way into my head, or was that avoidance? This wasn't really happening, was it? I shook my head slowly and tried to clutch onto something normal, safe. "I have work to do, photos to edit. I can't just leave." Not that I didn't want to find my brother, but this was beyond crazy. Was he really missing or was this some farce to kidnap me? Although I wasn't really kidnap material—there was no one rich who would pay ransom to get me back. Although, my parents hadn't been kidnap-worthy either, and they'd disappeared, and my brother? *Deep breaths, Lily.*

I bent and gathered the cup and lid. No matter how loopy things got, I wasn't a litterbug.

"You can edit the photos on your laptop on the plane or when we get to England. I could even have your desktop delivered, if you'd like. I know this is hard to believe. Just bear with me, and I'll explain everything while you're packing. Come on." She started walking towards my apartment block.

I shuffled along next to her, my legs heavy as if they were weighed down with lead boots. My gut told me she was telling the truth, so I concentrated on putting one foot in front of the other. I bit my lip to keep from crying again. Now wasn't the time to fall apart. My brother needed me.

And I never let down those I loved.

Never.

CHAPTER 3

As soon as the door shut back at my unit, I turned to Ma'am. "How do I know you're telling the truth? Anything could happen to me overseas. Are you for real?"

"Fair questions, I suppose. Why don't we call your sister-in-law? Give me your phone, so you know I'm not getting an imposter to talk to you."

I unlocked my phone and handed it to her. "Good luck. That thing hasn't been working properly. I tried calling her this morning, but I couldn't get through."

She grinned.

"What's so funny?"

"Have you had any other electricals stop working since yesterday?"

"Actually, yeah. My coffee machine died." The offending appliance sat uselessly in my kitchen, taking up valuable counter space and reminding me I'd only had half a cup of coffee today.

"It's to be expected—your power will intermittently interfere with things of that nature. You just turned twenty-four, the age when a witch's power comes in. Occasionally there are early bloomers, but it appears as if you're a normal witch. Your brother's power came in when he was twenty-two. He was more than ready, as he's very mature for his age. But from now on, you'll have to learn to contain your witchy energy."

I tried not to laugh. Okaaay. Among the other crazy things she'd said, she mentioned witch and normal in the same breath. Either she was totally loco, or she had the best poker-joke face ever. And was she insinuating I was immature? "Um, yep, that would be it. I was wondering when my powers would come in. It's about time, really." All jokes aside, James was more mature than me: that tended to happen when you took over looking after your sister when you were eighteen. He'd said no to a lot of parties and fun because of me. What if I never saw him again? Sadness wrapped familiar arms around me and squeezed.

"There's no need for sarcasm, my dear. I know this is a lot to take in, but you have to start sometime, and the sooner, the better. Your brother needs you." She pulled up my phone contacts, found Millicent, and pressed dial. "Millicent, dear, hello. Yes, it's Angelica. Yes, I'm here, but I need you to talk to her. I'm just going to put you on speaker. If Lily touches the phone, we'll lose the connection." She pressed a button.

Millicent's relieved voice poured from my phone. "Lily, it's me. Are you okay?"

"I think so. But is it true... about James?" My voice hitched. I couldn't lose my brother too.

"Yes. He was walking the dogs last Sunday, and he never came back. Pepper and Patty came home, their leads trailing behind them." Her voice quieted to almost a whisper, and I leaned forward to better hear what she was saying. "There was blood on their fur. Tests confirmed some was James's."

My heart raced. This couldn't be happening. "How much blood?"

"Enough that we knew it wasn't a scratch, but not enough that we could assume he'd bled out."

I swallowed and clutched my stomach. "Oh my God. I'm so sorry, Mill. You must be beside yourself. Why didn't you call me earlier in the week? You should have called."

"I was hoping he would've come back by now. I didn't want to scare you unnecessarily. Sorry we missed your birthday, but, well..."

Sheesh, she was going through hell, yet she was apologizing. I wanted to leap through the phone and give her a hug, even with my affection-aversion. "Oh my God, Mill. That's nothing. Forget about it. I'm here for you. In fact, soon I'll be there for you. Apparently, Ma'am has us on a flight out of Sydney today."

"I'm so glad I'll, finally meet you in person. Skype calls are good and all, but I need to give you a proper hug. Plus, you need to be here when we find James, because we *are* going to find him." Her deep intake of breath was clear down the phone line. "And I know the things Angelica has to say sound impossible, and even crazy, but you can trust her. I'm sorry about the timing, but I should let you know that I'm a witch too. Sorry to drop that on you and run, but I have to go. Love you, and I'll see you soon. Have a safe flight."

The line dropped out, and Angelica handed me the phone, not that it was much use in my witchy hands, apparently. Yeah, right. And Millicent was a witch too? This could not be happening. I didn't know if I was capable of believing this all—it was just too farfetched. I was a need-to-see-proof kind of person, hence my agnostic tendencies. I knew I couldn't prove anything about God or an afterlife one way or the other, so I stood in the middle, waiting for some kind of proof. Maybe it would never come, and I'd die and stop existing, never really knowing. Life really sucked. "Prove it."

"Prove that I'm a witch?"

"Yes, please. As if I'm going to fly halfway around the world with a stranger on just their word. Maybe you've threatened my sister-in-law too and made her say that stuff. Or maybe it's someone who sounds a lot like her."

"With her phone?"

"Well, you could have thugs at her place right now."

Angelica rolled her eyes. "If we must do this, fine."

Yes, we must.

She looked around the open-plan living area until her gaze stopped at my dining-room table, which was setup as my workstation. My desktop with two screens sat there surrounded by a pile of proofs, accounting paperwork, and mail in different stages of openness. Oh, and there was the half-finished bottle of Coke No Sugar I'd been looking for yesterday morning. Angelica looked at me and tsked.

"What? Being messy isn't a crime. I'm creative." I shrugged.

She blew out a loud breath and turned back towards my table. Her arms spread wide, and she chanted. *"So many things in a jumbled mess. Make it clean enough to impress."* Everything except for my computer disappeared then reappeared in an organised state. My mail was in a neat pile in a shoe-box-size organiser, the proofs were in a folder, and my accounting paperwork was neatly stacked to the right of the monitors. My mouth dropped open. Wow.

"There's no excuse to be messy."

"Not when you can do cool stuff like that, no, but I don't have time to be tidy. I can't just wave my arms around and spout poetry to make it happen." Just wow.

She raised a brow and tilted her head up. "Need any more proof?"

"No, I'm good. I don't think my brain can take any more hits to reality." Or what I'd thought was reality. If witches existed, did that mean vampires and werewolves did too? What, was I in a TV show now? Maybe it was Candid Camera. I looked around for hidden equipment.

"Good." She folded her arms, satisfaction oozing from every pore. She'd proven me wrong a couple of times already, and it wasn't even 10:00 a.m. People who always had to be right were kind of annoying. She smirked. "We need to get going, so we don't miss our flight. You'd best pack. I'll wait for you out here." She looked down at my sofa and brushed her palm against the cushion to move any potential debris out of the way before she sat. Rude much?

"Yeah, okay, but how much do I owe you for the flight?" I knew return flights were around eighteen hundred from Sydney to London; God knew I'd looked them up enough times. I'd been desperate to see my brother, but there never seemed to be a convenient time. Either I was short of cash, or he or I were too busy to spend the time we wanted if I made the effort to go all the way over there. That thousand-dollar tip from Mr Papadakis couldn't have come at a better time.

"You don't owe me anything. It's all taken care of."

"But, you can't pay for it. It's expensive."

"I'm not paying. The Paranormal Investigation Bureau is taking care of it."

"The what?"

"It's where I work. They're the ones investigating your brother's disappearance. They sent me here to fetch you. Now hurry along. We don't have much time."

Yep, things were getting stranger and stranger. When I went into my room, my suitcase was already splayed open on the bed. And stranger. I looked around. Had Angelica broken into my apartment while I was getting coffee earlier?

"No. I'm a witch. I asked it to happen, so it did. I was trying to save you time."

Goddammit! "Stay out of my head!" A snicker came

from my living room. Yeah, super funny. But hang on. "If you were trying to save me some time"—I called out—"then why didn't you pack my bag too?"

"Because I have no idea what you want to take, and I had no time to look through your things to pick appropriate clothing."

Hmm, so witches couldn't do everything *that* easily.

I changed my tights and sneakers for jeans and flat, black knee-high boots then hurriedly filled the case. Under-wear, check. Jeans, check. Jackets, check. Tracksuits, check. Four pairs of shoes for different weather, check. Toiletries, check. I squished my Ugg boots, pyjamas, and dressing gown onto the top and clipped the elastic thingies together to stop it from getting jumbled into a mess. I hauled the suit-case off my bed, and it thudded to the floor. I pulled the lever up and wheeled it out of my room. "How long will we be away?"

Ma'am was still perched on the edge of the sofa, her knees primly together, her back straight. "I don't think you'll be back any time soon."

"Oh." I hoped I wasn't gone too long. We needed to get James home as soon as possible, because he *wasn't* dead. Nope, not dead. I'd spend a little time with him then come back here. I had a wedding job booked in two weeks, and I really loved my apartment. It wasn't huge, but it was mine, bought with my share of my parents' life insurance. I almost felt like they were here with me. Plus, I had my friends, and the beach. Everything I loved, except my brother and his wife, was here.

I made sure my phone, wallet, headache tablets, iPod, iPad—coffee and Apple products were my weaknesses, oh… and camera lenses—laptop and passport were in my ruck-sack, gathered my camera equipment and struggled out the door. I must have been carting thirty kilos of stuff, which was equivalent to a medium-sized child, or a big dog. It would have been nice if Ma'am had helped. Couldn't she just magic my bags down the stairs? Come to think of it, I wouldn't say no to being magicked down the stairs either. *Did you hear that, Ma'am?*

"You're young. You can handle it," she called from the ground floor. I sighed.

The door clicked behind me. I checked it was locked and whispered, "Goodbye, home. I'll be back soon."

London, here I come.

CHAPTER 4

Angelica was Miss Super Organised. She'd booked us a cab that got us to the airport just in time for check in. The cab driver hoisted my bag out of the boot. A tingle, kind of like pins and needles, washed over my body. I shook it off then saddled myself with my plethora of bags. I turned to Angelica, who was standing there holding a handbag and small carry-on with wheels. Huh? Where did they come from?

She leant close, speaking quietly. "We're travelling internationally. A passenger with no luggage would draw unwanted attention." She had a point. But where did the bags come from? Yeah, I get it was magic, but *how*? And if I was a witch—*yeah, right*—was I capable of doing that too? Maybe when they were recruiting witches, they should explain all the fun stuff first.

Angelica seemed relaxed and not like someone who was

about to suffer for hours on end. Maybe she'd just magic herself and sleep the whole way? But I was magickless, or at least incompetent when it came to that, so I wasn't looking forward to cattle class. Economy travel was just another name for torture. With two flights and a stopover totalling around twenty-four hours, I'd have plenty of time to stew in my misery. I'd done the flight once with my family, when I was eleven. We'd visited my dad's family in Italy, and it was amazing once we got there, but sitting upright and sleepless for so long was not something I'd forget in a hurry. I envied those people who could sleep sitting up. Bastards.

Imagine my joy when we breezed through the non-existent line for business class. My mouth dropped open. No freaking way! *I get a bed! Woohoo!*

"Don't stand there gawking, dear. Place your bag onto the scales, please." Angelica's bemusement spread across her face in a large grin. Who knew she could actually look not in the least bit scary?

We grabbed our tickets and headed for security. By the time we made it through there, I was hungry and in need of another coffee. It was a wonder I'd made it this far on only half a cup.

"We can get you some coffee in the Qantas lounge."

Ooh, I get to use the lounge as well. This was awesome. I smiled, but it was short lived when I remembered why we were there.

"Take happiness where you find it, Lily. You'll never get this day back again, even if it's not the best day. I'm sure James would want you relaxed and ready to do all you can to help find him when we get there. Enjoy this while you can."

"Okay. I'll try. Also, can you stop reading my mind, please? It almost feels like I'm naked in front of you." Was she even capable of it, or was it like trying not to hear conversations that were happening right next to you?

"I can switch off, but I needed to know where you're at —you know, in case you lose the plot and have a breakdown or something."

I stopped and stared at her. I ground my back teeth together. *What the actual...?* She stopped at the same time, probably reading my mind. Again. I was careful to keep my voice a decibel quieter than normal, so there was no mistaking whether I was losing my mind. "If anyone has the right to lose the plot, it's me. Do you know what I've been through in the last twenty-four hours? I'd say I'm doing pretty freaking well considering. Now get out of my head."

She placed her palms on my head, mumbled a few words that sent shivers over my body, then she stepped back. "It's done. You're protected. Now no one can listen into your thoughts." By no one, she meant no witches, but that would have sounded strange to any normal person walking past.

I tested a thought and made sure it was surprising and loud. Oh my God! Look out! Huh, no reaction. She was probably telling the truth. We resumed walking. "Can all you-know-whats read minds?"

"No. It's a skill that has to be learned, and not everyone has the aptitude. There are many different skills we can have, but it's like normal people. Some are good at carpentry or maths, while some are good at teaching or speaking multiple languages. There are some things practically all of us can learn to do—like travelling and materialising things."

"Like with my suitcase today?"

"Yes. But you can't just conjure something up that has never existed. We can only move tangible things from one place to another. And if you were to conjure a dress out of a store without paying, for instance, you'd be committing a crime. That's some of what the PIB deal with."

The PIB? *Oh, that's right, the Paranormal Investigation Bureau. Interesting.*

We arrived at the Qantas lounge and signed in. *Luxury, here I come.* I'd heard all sorts of good things about airport lounges from one of my friends, Michelle. She worked for an airline and got cheap flights plus lounge admittance. Apparently, you could eat and drink as much as you wanted of what was on offer, including alcohol, and coffee. I grinned and headed straight for the barista.

Once I'd grabbed my large skim-milk cappuccino and cheese-and-ham croissant, I settled into the private booth Angelica had chosen. It was at one end of the lounge, in the corner, for the most part away from unwanted ears.

"Where will I be staying once we get there?" I bit through the crunchy, light pastry and hit melted cheese and ham, the salty tastiness bursting through my mouth. "Mmm."

"Millicent has offered for you to stay there, but I don't

think that's a good idea. I'd prefer if you stayed with me, at the PIB safe house. It's guarded against normal and not-so-normal threats. Plus, you have a lot to learn, and we'll have plenty of space and privacy to work on your special skills there."

That's right. When I'd first met Angelica, she'd said she was my teacher *and* my protector, although I couldn't see her decking anyone with her slim-boned fists, and I didn't think she liked me enough to take a bullet for me. Maybe she could magic people dead? That could work. "Am I in danger?"

She sipped her tea—typical Brit fare—then placed her cup on the saucer with not a hint of noise. Impressive. Her expression became guarded. "Maybe. There've been no direct threats." She picked her tea up again and held it to her lips. Was she hiding behind her teacup? Not much of a protector.

"But..."

She shrugged. I sipped my coffee and swallowed my frustration. "What sort of things do you think I could do with my... talents?"

She placed her cup down, and her face relaxed. We were obviously in safer territory. "Well, your mother could tell the future, and your brother is good at truth-seeing." Wow, there were so many things I needed to ask.

"What about my dad? And did you know my mother? What's truth-seeing?"

Angelica laughed. "Your father was normal in the sense that he had no supernatural talents, but he was a black belt in three different martial arts and knew his way around weapons. He was your mother's protector."

Mind. Blown. My father was a history teacher, not a ninja. I'd never seen him be the least bit aggressive, except when he yelled at me to clean my room.

"Your mother could see the future, sometimes, but her talent never gave her a clear picture of things. It was more clues that she'd have to piece together. As for truth-seeing, your brother can tell when someone's lying. He can also wipe people's memories down to a specific minute."

My face must have shown my horror, because Angelica smirked. "Don't worry; his powers hadn't come in when you were living together. Any little fibs you told him as a child would have gone undiscovered."

I blushed. I wasn't a pathological liar or anything, but one day I'd borrowed his favourite skateboard. He'd told me I could use any of his five skateboards except one, and yep, that one was the one I coveted. There's nothing more attractive than something you can't have, especially if it had a shiny red skull on it. I'd ridden it down a hill—okay, probably more incline than hill—and I lost control at the bottom. I jumped off, just saving my arse, but his board sped into a roadside drain, and the grate was too heavy for my nine-year-old self to move, so I had to leave it there. I was too scared to tell anyone, so it was never recovered. I'm sure he suspected I'd taken it, but I denied everything, little shit that I was.

And he repaid me by looking after me after our parents

disappeared. I didn't deserve him. If... no, *when* we found him, I was totally going to 'fess up.

"If my mum could sort of see the future, why did they still go to England that time?" If Angelica knew my family's history, which it seemed like she did, she would know that's where they disappeared—supposedly at a history conference my father had attended.

"She didn't like to see her future. Your mother stopped using her talents when you were about five. I understand there were things she saw that came true—the deaths of your grandparents for instance—and she didn't want to know anymore. She wanted to just enjoy her life with her children. She used to work with me, you know. Before I ran the training division, we were both in investigations. You look a lot like her—same gorgeous auburn hair and olive skin. Your eyes are the same sky-blue, too."

I hardly ever got compared to either of my parents, because no one I knew now had known them. Sometimes, if my friends checked out the family photos around my apartment, they'd mention something, but it was hard to tell from such small mementos. Her compliment was bittersweet. "Thanks. I never get to hear that. You said my mother was a detective?"

"In the PIB, yes."

"She never even hinted she'd done anything like that. Why would she hide it?" A funny feeling I didn't like squirmed through my body. It was more than sadness, more than disappointment and confusion. For the first time, I wondered if I'd really known my mother at all. I only knew about the life she'd had with me and my brother. "Do you think it was her special talents that got her kidnapped or murdered?" I held my breath. I'd never said the *M* word out loud before, but of course I'd thought it. Everyone I knew had; we were all just too chicken to say it. I swallowed a mass of fear pushing against my throat.

"She had her reasons for not saying anything. Anyway, we're not here to solve your parents' disappearance. We need to find James, and I think there's a good chance he's alive. Not all the blood on his dogs belonged to him. A fair amount came from two people we have yet to identify. Also, Millicent thinks she can still sense him, which might just be a wife's wishful thinking, but stranger things have happened."

Oh, stranger things, like opening your door on a Monday morning to find out you're a witch and your brother's disappeared? Yep, if today is anything to go by, anything is possible. Why couldn't the anything be good stuff, like a bag full of money or a hot guy with morals and intelligence turning up on my doorstep? Because: real life.

I finished my croissant and coffee and dug my ticket out of my bag to check our departure time. An hour and a half to go. I didn't think finding out anything else right now would be beneficial to my mental health, so I took my Nikon out of my bag. Angelica had pulled a mystery book from her bag and was reading. "I'm going to snap some shots. I'll be back in thirty minutes."

"Don't get lost."

"I'll try not to. See you soon."

When I was behind a camera, I was in my happy place. I wandered the airport and found an alcove set back from the main thoroughfare. With my camera poised in front of my face, I glimpsed the travellers through the lens. A balding man in a blue shirt, top button undone, brown brief-case swinging from his arm marched towards his flight. *Click, click.* An older couple, slowly wheeling their carry-on behind them, made their careful way to another flight. Age spots peppered his wrinkled face. *Click, click.* Were they visiting family or friends, or were they headed home? A middle-aged man in an INXS T-shirt—that was a blast from the past—laughed with his two mates. Tattoos snaked down his arms. His mate slapped his back as they passed. *Click, click.* I was about to swap focus to someone else, when he faded out, as in went all see through, like Mr Papadakis had done last night. I clicked, just to make sure there was nothing wrong with my camera. Maybe my powers were affecting it?

I lowered my camera as they moved away. Without my camera in the way, he was as solid as everyone else. Maybe I was losing it? I pressed the button to look at the photos on the camera screen. Nausea squeezed my stomach. I switched back and forth from the last photo to the second last. In one, he was solid, but in the other, he had faded, and I could see the garbage bin and another person that had been behind him, out of my line of sight. What did this mean? My camera wasn't broken. No camera could see through things, except for an X-ray. Maybe there was some-thing going on with the exposure?

I gave up. So much for some downtime. Maybe I should just return to the lounge and read. I had a few books on my iPad Kindle app that I was looking forward to reading. That would distract me.

As I reached the Qantas lounge sign-in counter, just outside the entrance doors, my phone rang. I stopped and pulled it out of my back pocket. Would it work? Stuffed if I knew, but I'd soon find out. I swiped across and put the phone to my ear. "Hello, Lily speaking."

The voice on the other end was clear. I was relieved for all of two seconds, until I heard who it was. "Hi, Lily." She sniffed and hiccupped. "It's Tracy, the… the bride from last night." Was she crying? "Um, I wanted to ask if I could have all the photos of my dad from the wedding."

"Of course. Even if they're no good?"

"Yes." A small sob came down the line. She was definitely crying.

"Are you okay?" She hadn't been the nicest of people last night, but I hated seeing anyone upset.

"Um, no." Her voice squeaked up a pitch, and she hiccupped again. "I'd like all the photos of my dad, because he… he died this morning."

My breath stuck in my throat, and my heart hammered as a prickle zapped down my spine. "I'm so sorry. Oh my God. He was such a lovely man." I wanted to know how he'd died, but I didn't think asking was the appropriate thing to do. Wanting to know was an awkward but legitimate response, if you asked me.

She cried for a moment then drew in a loud breath.

"Thanks. Yes, he was. I don't know what we're going to do without him, but if you could just send me his photos, even before any of the others, I'd really appreciate it."

"Will do. I'm just about to board a flight, but I'll get them to you in the next couple of days."

"Thanks. Bye." She hung up. I turned my camera back on and scrolled through the photos from last night. My heart didn't slow as I passed photo after photo. Until I got to Mr Papadakis. I hadn't imagined it. He was see through. Oh, crap. I thought he'd looked like a ghost, and now he was dead. Was it a coincidence? If it wasn't, that guy with the tats didn't have long to live, according to my Nikon.

Was this my special power?

A wave of vomit surged up my throat. I barely registered the look of horror on the lounge attendant's pretty face before I threw up all over the floor.

Happy freaking birthday, Lily. Twenty-four was going to be a killer year, but not in the way I wanted.

I puked again.

CHAPTER 5

We'd been in the air for two hours, and my brain had finally stopped running in circles screaming. Before we boarded, Angelica had created some kind of witchy shield around me, so my energy wouldn't cause havoc with the plane controls or navigation. I was glad she was here to warn me. What if I'd gone on holidays not knowing? I could have been the cause of hundreds of deaths. Warning letters should be sent to all witches on their twenty-fourth birthday. Not that I would have believed it, although, considering all the other electrical problems I'd had, I may have.

The quiet hum of the engine was reassuring. I relaxed into my wide leather seat and glanced around at the other elegant, chilled passengers in their luxurious I'm-also-a-bed-suck-on-that-economy-passengers seats. I could get used to this.

Angelica looked up from her book. "How are you feeling?"

"Better. Thanks. I think the last twenty-four hours finally caught up with me." I hadn't told her what had set me off. I wanted to process it before I told anyone. I could be wrong anyway. Also, not that I didn't trust her, but I didn't know her very well, and I wasn't sure I wanted her knowing everything about me. I would share my secrets when I felt more comfortable. "I wonder what the suckers in economy are up to?" If I were being honest, business class was more enjoyable because I knew I had it better than the other poor sods. Yes, I used to be one of those sods, and probably would be again, but for now, I was queen of this plane. I grinned.

"I imagine they're reading or watching a movie. Nothing out of the ordinary. Why do they interest you?" There was that poker face again. Was she serious?

"They don't. Not really. It was a rhetorical question." Way to ruin my fun.

"Is there anything else you'd like to talk about?" She looked at me expectantly. She could look as long as she liked, but I wasn't ready to share. *Nope.*

"No, thank you. I'm good. I might get some of that photo editing done. My client's eager to get her wedding photos back."

"I'm here if you need to talk. Lily…" The shallow lines on her forehead smoothed out, and her gaze softened. "I'm on your side. You can't trust everyone you come across, and I do advise caution, but you can trust me and Millicent. If you need anything, let one of us know." In that moment, I believed her, and I knew I'd open up to her, just not today.

"Thank you. That means a lot." I was used to only relying on myself, or my brother at a pinch. Leaning on others would take some getting used to, but if me opening up to more people helped find James, I was in. There was nothing I wouldn't do to find him.

I stuck my iPod earphones in and opened my laptop.

The rest of the flight to Dubai, our stopover, was pretty damn awesome, except now I was ruined for economy. After we got back on the plane, I changed into my cute Qantas-issue grey business-class pyjamas. They had a dark blue flying kangaroo motif. I was so taking them with me when we landed—unexpected free stuff was awesome. I lay in my Skybed and grinned—I was worried about James, but I may never be this comfortable or pampered again, so I was going to appreciate the moment. I shut my eyes, and within ten minutes, old-man sleep took my hand and led me down the rabbit hole.

Before I knew it, we were landing at Heathrow, where the next part of my journey would begin.

I just hoped today started off better than yesterday, because if it didn't, I was in a whole world of trouble.

❦

I'D NEVER BEEN TO ENGLAND, AND AS OUR BLACK Mercedes, replete with smartly suited and capped driver—the PIB did everything in style, apparently—drove from the airport through the countryside to the south, I stared out the window, taking it all in. We'd arrived in the early morning to fog and light drizzle, but I didn't care: I was in England, in a luxury car, and I didn't have to drive. Bonus! There were, of course, thoughts of my brother and parents swirling around in my head, creating a backdrop of melancholy that under-pinned my mood, but a bit of excitement and wonder at being here did seep through.

Angelica sat with me in the back. She'd made a couple of phone calls but now stared out the window, her hands neatly arranged in her lap. Her clothes weren't wrinkled, and there wasn't a wisp of light-brown hair out of place. The bun-of-death gripped it all in an unrelenting show of dominance. How that didn't give her a headache was beyond me. I, on the other hand, had a messy, loose pony-tail, tendrils of hair falling to the sides of my face, annoying me. My T-shirt had a stain on the front from where I'd spilled a splotch of coffee during turbulence, but the weather was cool, and I hid it with my black jumper.

We were headed south of London, to the village of Westerham in Kent. I couldn't wait to see the area where my brother lived. The few photos he'd sent showed charac-ter-filled towns, and I loved old buildings. Weddings were what I photographed to earn money, but my true love was photographing nature and architecture. Sydney had some nice late-nineteenth- and early-twentieth-century buildings, but that was the exception rather than the norm. I couldn't wait to explore.

I pulled my phone out of my bag and turned it on. My

power was still contained, as far as I was aware, so it should work. In the disaster that was yesterday, I forgot to let at least one of my friends know I was out of the country —not that I had any pets or plants to keep alive. It was nice to be the traveller and not the friend staying home listening to someone else's stories for a change—Michelle got to go to so many awesome places. I pulled up my messages and found the last one I sent to her and wrote another one.

Me: Hey, chicky. Just off to London for spring fashion week. Hanging out with my super-fabulous rich friends LOL. Just kidding, well not about the going to London bit. My brother's sick, and I had savings, so I decided on a last-minute trip. Not sure when I'll be back, but I'll keep you updated. Don't be too jealous ;). Cheers xx.

I would have loved to brag about travelling business class, but I wasn't ready to answer any of the questions that would initiate. "Ah, crap!" I hadn't turned on roaming. I quickly turned my phone to airplane mode. I probably owed my telephone company seven hundred dollars for that slip-up.

"What's wrong, dear?" Angelica was looking at me, concern on her face.

"Nothing. I just have to set up roaming on my phone or grab a UK SIM card."

"We can do that once we get your things put away at home. If you behave, I'll buy you a cappuccino." She graced me with smile, which she'd been stingy with the whole time I'd known her. Was smiling something she normally avoided, or was I special?

"I think I can manage that. How much longer till we get there?"

"Another fifteen minutes or so. I'm going to take the shield off your powers now."

I scrunched my face, anticipating the worst.

"It won't hurt." She shook her head as if she couldn't believe what an idiot she was dealing with. So much for smiling Angelica. My scalp tingled momentarily. "Done."

Hmm, so she was right. Go figure. Normally when adults told kids it wouldn't hurt, it was a big fat lie to get them to hold still—think inoculations or Band-Aid removal. Yes, I was fully aware I wasn't a child, but that was how Angelica made me feel, and in terms of witch experience, I was a newborn.

We turned off the highway onto a secondary road that wound through low-lying hills. It was single lane each way and narrow, even though there was a reasonable amount of traffic. Fields gave way to hedgerows within one metre of the shoulder. I eagerly waited for breaks in the foliage. Every now and then a whitewashed Tudor mansion or smaller stone cottage flashed into view.

Soon hedges and fields changed to two-storey houses, some even on the street front, so close to the road that passing buses must have rattled their windows. This had all been built way before cars, when traffic jams consisted of a line of horses and carts.

"The village was established in the thirteenth century,

although there is evidence of some earlier settlement. Winston Churchill lived here for many years. Have you heard of him?"

"Wasn't he some fat guy who owned a sweet shop?"

Her eyes widened in definite horror. I laughed. "Just joking. I'm not an idiot. He was your prime minister during the Second World War. He was the one who brought in the eight-hour working day and minimum wage, and he said cool things like 'The price of greatness is responsibility.'" Hmm, I knew more about him than I thought.

"You surprise me."

I surprised myself. "The benefits of having a history teacher for a father." Right then, I missed Dad so much. He would have loved to have been here to share this moment with me, and he would have had so much to tell me about Westerham and Churchill in that enthusiastic way of his where his eyes shone and he waved his arms to emphasise everything.

We passed through the centre of the town; shingles, dark brick, and chimneys abounded. Some of the buildings were over five hundred years old. This was so cool. The Tudor style—white cladding standing out against dark timber— was gorgeous, with one row of conjoined buildings housing an interior design shop, wine bar, and a dress shop. It went by too fast to see more details, but I'd definitely come up here later and have a wander around. I also wanted to catch up with Millicent.

After zipping through town, we turned right, down an even narrower street, the driver slowing to let a car going the opposite way pass. Cottages lined the street, some I could just see behind vibrant green hedges, some visible in their full character-filled glory over a low fence. Window planter boxes bursting with spring blooms gave a shot of colour.

What would the PIB house look like? I hoped it was old but not haunted. Speaking of which, poor Mr Papadakis. I wondered how he died, and if I could have prevented it if I'd known what my camera was trying to tell me. If it turned out I was having premonition-type experiences, what was I supposed to do with them? Why have them if I wasn't supposed to do anything? Bummer. I really needed to talk to someone, but I wasn't ready to talk to Angelica. Maybe Millicent could help?

The blinker clicked its lulling rhythm, and we turned left into a gravel driveway that ran under a canopy of branches. We pulled up at the end, in front of a stunning three-storey Tudor home. I got out of the car and stared. The ground floor was red brick with black-framed timber windows, then the first floor was white cladding with uneven dark timber crisscrossed through it, then the top floor comprised of the cutest dormer windows surrounded by reddish shingles. I took my phone out of my pocket and snapped a few shots.

"Is there Wi-Fi here?" I asked Angelica who was already at the front door, sans bags. I guessed there was no premise to keep up here, so she'd ditched them. Half her luck. I turned to grab my bag, but the driver waved me away. "I'll take care of these, Miss."

"Oh, thanks. Are you sure?"

"Positive." He gave a single nod. So reserved.

Angelica called out from inside. "Yes, we have it. I'll give you the password later. Surely you can live without your device for five minutes?"

I bit my tongue. I didn't need to remind her that I'd hardly used it since I'd met her; in fact, I wasn't that attached to my phone. I did love Instagram, but I hardly communicated with anyone. I preferred to see people in the flesh rather than have marathon messaging sessions, and my Facebook was full of people who had to share what they had for dinner, their latest trip to the hospital, or what amazing thing their four-year-old just did. I needed new Facebook friends. Surely there were more interesting people out there?

I walked through the thickly framed front door into a high-ceilinged vestibule, my footsteps clicking on the polished timber floors. A staircase sat against the far wall, its glossy timber banister curling around as it ascended past framed portraits. Stone-framed doorways led to the left and right.

Angelica came down the staircase and stopped halfway down. "Well, are you coming up? I want to show you your room."

"Ah, yes, sure." She was quick. I hadn't even seen where she'd gone. Maybe she "popped" up there magically? I followed her to the top floor where she showed me to a bedroom with exposed beams and a dormer window.

The floor creaked as I entered, and I detected the distinct odour of eucalyptus furniture polish. Whitewashed bedside tables with sixties-style lamps stood on either side of the mahogany bedhead. It was a queen-size bed, thank goodness. A thick, white quilt embroidered with delicate lavender flowers adorned the bed. *Nice.*

"There's a shower on this floor, and a towel on your bed. Why don't you shower and meet me downstairs in fifteen minutes?"

"Okay." Angelica left. I looked around for my bag. It wasn't here yet. A small vibration disturbed the air, and it appeared at the end of my bed. I jumped. For the love of all that's holy. I put my hand to my chest. Jeepers. Wasn't it dangerous to just move stuff somewhere you couldn't see? What if I'd been sitting there? That wasn't very sensible. Yet another question to ask Angelica.

I grabbed the stuff I needed and went to find cleanliness. The sooner I showered, the sooner I could help find James.

I'D DRESSED IN BLACK JEANS, BLACK LONG-SLEEVE T-SHIRT, hiking boots and my thick black jumper. I had a beanie in my pocket, just in case. When I made it to the ground floor, I called out tentatively. "Angelica? Hello?"

Her cultured voice rang out from the hallway to my right. "In here, dear."

I found a door that led into a large living room that was divided into two separate areas by furniture placement. Light filtered in through the lattice-patterned windows, the sun forming criss-crosses on the windowsill and floor. The ceiling was lower than I expected, maybe a foot lower than at home, although it made it feel cosy. Two blue Persian rugs lay on the floor—one at either end of the room. I couldn't love this room any more than I did. It was perfect.

Two three-seat oxblood-red leather Chesterfield couches faced each other in one area, and in the other, two armchairs faced the crackling fire. Two people sat on one of the Chesterfields, their backs to me.

"Lily!" Before I could react, Millicent jumped up off the sofa, hurried over, and enveloped me in a hug. I hugged her back.

"Are you okay, Mill?" I leaned back to check her out. Her skin was pale, but that wasn't unusual—she was English, and they'd just been through winter. Her blonde hair sat straight and glossy to her shoulders, but her eyes were red-rimmed. She had on a pink cashmere sweater. She was always so demure and dressed the part—at least from what I'd seen from Skype and photos. "Any news?"

She shook her head. "But I'm so glad you're here. You can help us find him. I know you can." I hoped she was right. "I heard your powers came in." She smiled, and wrinkles formed at the corners of her eyes.

"Apparently, but I have no idea what I can do or how to do it. I'm not sure if it's polite to ask, but what can you do?"

"Aside from the normal conjuring cups of tea and things, and travelling, I can communicate with animals, but in pictures rather than words, and I can see in the dark."

Huh. That last one sounded more like a superhero ability. Also, didn't we have torches for that? Not knocking her abilities, mind you, but I hoped mine were more useful than seeing in the dark. "If you can communicate with animals, were you able to get any information out of your dogs when they came back without James?"

"Yes." She took a deep breath. "Pepper showed me a white hand that had a snake tattoo and a thick gold masculine ring with a square emerald stone in the centre. He didn't see the attacker's face, as he wore a balaclava. Patty bit another person on the leg, and she indicated it tasted like garlic—I cook bolognaise with garlic, no onion mind you, as the dogs are allergic, and she showed me the bolognaise sauce in her mind, and then I had to show her the different ingredients until she pawed at the garlic."

"Wow, that's amazing." I wasn't even being sarcastic, although I wasn't sure it was a genuine clue. Did the dog understand, or had she just decided to raise her paw at that time for no particular reason?

"And Patty brought back a piece of fabric that she'd ripped from the guy's trousers."

Angelica stood from the sofa and approached us. "We have that in an evidence bag at PIB headquarters."

"So how am I supposed to help? I don't know anything about detective work or how to use my witch skills. I feel like I'm just going to get in the way." I huffed out a frustrated breath.

Millicent looked to Angelica with raised brows, but Angelica gave nothing away, poker face that she was. Maybe she'd overdosed on Botox recently? She smirked at me. That dirty, rotten…

"I thought you'd blocked my thoughts."

Angelica shrugged. "It wears off after twelve hours or so."

"Do you do this to everyone, or are my thoughts incredibly fascinating?"

"I can't read everyone's mind all the time—that would be like trying to listen to every conversation at a party at once. Besides, most witches can block their thoughts."

I folded my arms. "When can you teach me?"

Angelica pursed her lips, probably considering my question. "I'm not sure. We need to take things slowly and make sure we protect you from yourself." Way to inspire confidence.

"Can't you just tell me what to do, and if I think I can't handle it, I'll wait to learn more before I try?" Surely I couldn't be that bad. I was usually a fast learner, and I knew my limits.

Angelica shook her head. "If you get this spell wrong, you could squeeze your brain too tight and give yourself a migraine, or even permanent brain damage."

That didn't sound good. I was about to acquiesce when Millicent said, "Oh, come on, Angelica. It's not that hard. You're scaring the poor girl."

"Very well, then, but don't say I didn't warn you."

"You don't have to. I mean, if it's that dangerous, maybe I should wait."

Millicent gave me an encouraging smile. "Don't worry. You'll be fine. I wouldn't have said anything if I thought you were incapable. You are descended from the Ashworths.

They were one of the strongest witch families around before their line almost died out. You and your brother are the last of the witchy Ashworths."

I had cousins on my father's side—they lived in Italy—but none on my mother's. My mother had had a brother and sister, but they'd both died in their teens. She hadn't liked to talk about what had happened, so I never pried.

"Well, let's get my education started. I wouldn't want to let the Ashworth name down." Butterflies flitted about inside my stomach. My brave face was all for show. What if I was crap? What if the skill was dependent upon my belief in magic? I was new to all this, and I wasn't 100 per cent onboard with the believing thing.

Millicent sat on one of the Chesterfields, and Angelica and I sat on the other. I took a deep breath and looked at my mentor, her back straight and a no-nonsense expression on her face. Was this really happening? This was so freaking crazy, yet here I was.

"You may not get it the first few times, but don't worry. Like anything, magic takes practice. And I expect you to practice, but only when Millicent or I are present. I'll remind you that it can be dangerous when you don't know what you're doing. Do you understand?"

"Yes, Ma'am."

"Good. Now, close your eyes. You won't always have to, but it will help you focus by cutting out any distractions. I want you to imagine an invisible bubble around your brain. Think about it until you know the bubble inside and out. Make sure to leave a small gap between the bubble and your brain, or you'll do yourself an injury, and, in order for it to work properly, the barrier mustn't have any holes. Concentrate."

I was concentrating, imagining an invisible bubble. Hang on, if it was invisible, how could I tell if it had holes?

"Okay, smarty pants, make it blue."

"I just think you should have thought about it before you went about teaching people, Ma'am."

"I rarely teach, but when I do, the student is normally smart enough to keep up."

Angelica 1, me 0.

"If you're done being the clown, check your *blue* bubble has no holes, and then I want you to repeat after me. *These thoughts are mine; I do not wish to share. Protect them well, little bubble, with a barrier a little bluer than air.*"

The words didn't sound as magical in my Australian accent. When I uttered the last word, a tingle warmed my scalp, and I heard one strike of what sounded like a very cute bell. The pure, high note lasted for barely two seconds. I opened my eyes and looked around, although I didn't know what I imagined would have changed, the bubble being in my skull and invisible to the human eye.

Angelica smiled and nodded. "Very well done, Lily! You did it."

I looked at Millicent. "Did it work?"

She shrugged, a very demure lift of her petite shoulders. "I'm not sure. I can't read minds... well, not human ones."

"You'll just have to take my word for it. A novel concept,

wouldn't you agree?" Angelica tilted her head and gave me a look that had probably felled lesser people.

No sense letting her wallow in her anger. "What do we do now? Are there other things I need to learn? Also, what if I get one of the words wrong. Does something bad happen?" My memory could be crap. Maybe I'd need to write all these spells down, but in an emergency, it wasn't like I'd have time to find them in my bag, pull them out and read them. Looked like studying would be in my near future.

"It depends. If you get a word wrong and there isn't a spell with that word, probably nothing will happen, or, if it's close enough to the word you changed, it may work. But if you change the words and accidentally make a different spell, there could be terrible consequences. When you're experienced, you can create your own spells, although testing a spell out for the first time is dangerous. One never knows what might happen." Angelica laughed. Wow, it took the thought of catastrophe to cheer her up. This was all a bit too serious.

"I know I need a lot of training, but I'd really like to find James." I glanced at Millicent. Her shoulders tensed. How was she holding it together? I resisted the urge to jump out of my seat, shake someone, and shout, "Why aren't we doing something?" James needed us now. If I thought about it much longer without doing anything to find him, I would lose it, like ear-piercing scream and ripping my hair out of my head, crazy-town lose it. "I mean, the longer we take to find him, the worse it is for him. Right?" I didn't want to say what we were all probably thinking—the longer we took to find him, the greater the chance he'd be the *D* word. I wouldn't entertain that thought, but unease slithered across my scalp. I shivered. "Have you got any leads at all?"

Millicent looked at the ground and sighed.

"You must have something!" I stood.

Angelica raised her head so her nose was in the air, and she pursed her lips, all the while staring me down. "Of course we do. We have clues from the dogs. We have a cast of tyre tracks from near where he was taken, the blood from the dogs, and we're currently looking at all the cases he's worked since he joined PIB. Your family line produced intelligent, strong witches—your brother is exceptionally gifted at what he does. We were hoping you would have inherited power that could help us. Your mother could read the future, after all."

"So, if I wasn't a witch, you wouldn't have brought me here?"

Millicent blushed, but she met my gaze. "Probably not. No."

"Would you have even told me he was missing?"

Angelica stood and placed her hands on her hips. "Not until it was absolutely necessary, and you never would have met me. The PIB is a secret organisation. No non-witches, except for high-clearance government officials, know about our organisation. We help solve normal crimes too, but we deal with any transgressions perpetrated by witches or where witches are victims. If you really want to help, you need to discover your talents, and quickly."

Oh, no pressure then. I swallowed the lump in my throat. There was so much I didn't know about the case or being a witch. Maybe I could help them with my awesome logic skills until I figured out what the deal was with my powers. I didn't want to fess up about the camera thing. It was no use since there were no strangers here to take a picture of. The anomaly had only shown up on live subjects. Maybe I needed to do more homework on what I could do. "The town centre isn't far. Do you mind if I take a walk, soak all this culture in? I wouldn't mind grabbing a coffee and some lunch, take some photos. Maybe if I relax a bit, I can figure out what I can do?"

The two women exchanged a look, then Angelica spoke. "I don't like the idea of you wandering around by yourself, but very well. I have to go into headquarters this afternoon. Millicent can stay here in case you need one of us urgently. Be careful, and don't get lost."

Would it be childish of me to point out I was an adult? "I'll be careful, and I'll try not to get lost. I'll just follow the scent of coffee to the nearest café. And if I'm not back in two hours, Millicent can come find me." I smiled. "Oh, in all the madness, I didn't get a chance to change any money. Will my card work in the ATM or will my powers interfere?"

Angelica placed her palms on my shoulders and mumbled something. Warmth spread over my skin. "I've shielded you again. It's probably for the best as it hides you from other witches too."

"Huh?"

"Witches give off a signal when they perform magic. I

was alerted on your birthday, when your power started. Can you tell me what happened?"

I kept a straight face—at least, I hoped I did. "I didn't do any spells. Nothing happened until the next morning, when my coffee machine blew." *Liar, liar pants on fire.* I hoped one of her skills wasn't lie detecting. Although technically, I didn't consciously do anything—it had just happened.

She raised her brow. "Magic can be passive or active. The passive side is what happens without us trying; you could call it your natural talent—James's lie detecting would be an example. The active magic is the spells we cast, where we actively change things." Out of all the examples she could have used....

I shrugged. "Nothing that I noticed. Anyway, I'd love to get out there and see how I can help. I guess I'll see you both later?" I smiled.

Angelica regarded me but left it alone. Maybe she'd heard my thoughts earlier and already knew. Even so, surely she'd understand I needed to figure this out before I went telling people stuff. What if it was a camera fault and I got everyone's hopes up for nothing?

"Bye, sweetie." Millicent gave me another hug. That's it: I was out of hugs for the week. "I'll see you back here this afternoon, and we can go over any new information Angelica finds out at the Bureau. And be careful."

Was this place more dangerous than they were letting on? That was two serious "be carefuls". "Sounds good. I promise I'll have something to share with you this afternoon, even if it isn't great."

Angelica gave a curt nod, and Millicent smiled. Looked like I was going to cave at giving her some information earlier than I thought. Not a comforting thought. "Bye!"

I shrugged off the tiredness of travel and bolted upstairs to grab my camera, beanie, and wallet, before racing back down again. A mixture of excitement and fear coagulated in my stomach. In order to save my brother, I had to find out who I really was, but before any great expedition, there must be coffee. At least that was one problem I could solve without getting into too much trouble.

CHAPTER 6

The aroma of freshly brewed coffee and English-accented chatter filled the Costa café. Dim lighting and warm browns and oranges created a cosy atmosphere. I sipped my cappuccino and soaked it all in. It was only ten degrees outside, and most people who walked past wore jackets, but some wore only a T-shirt and jeans. What was this madness? I supposed some people could acclimatise to anything. It was toasty inside, though, so my beanie sat on the table next to my camera and incredible double chocolate muffin. I'd eaten the top off, and runny chocolate oozed from the middle. If this wasn't heaven, I didn't know what was.

I alternated mouthfuls of decadent sweetness and coffee until it was all gone. *So good.* I licked my fingers and smiled. I loved England. Okay, so I'd hardly seen any of it yet, but I thought it was my spirit home—like having a spirit animal but it's home instead. Made total sense.

Now I'd finished, it was time to go outside and explore, which was both terrifying and exciting. I wanted so badly to look around and capture the village through my lens, but what if I saw more soon-to-be-dead people? If that's what they really were. Not knowing meant I couldn't warn them, and even if I could warn them, did I want to be seen as a lunatic? Because, really, what else would they think?

I picked my camera up and caressed it with my thumb. Holding my camera was as natural as breathing. When I didn't have it in my hands, it felt like something was missing, and if I went somewhere without it, I suffered the nagging desperation most people experienced when they forgot their phone. It really was an extension of me. I loved that I could show people a different version of the world—a distilled version that somehow conveyed so much more than when looking at something with the naked eye.

As much as I wanted to put this off, I needed to figure it out, because not using my camera ever again was not an option. Come to think of it, I wondered if my phone would have the same results. Was it the camera itself—still a possibility—or was it me using it? Could a camera be haunted? I laughed. That made just as much sense as everything else I'd experienced in the last day, so why not.

My parents had given me my first instant camera. I had them to thank for the gift of having a passion to follow. On my sixteenth birthday, James had given me my first "proper" camera. It was a second-hand Nikon D3000, although it wasn't quite a year old, so it was almost new. It was the best present ever. I didn't use it anymore, but I still had it at home—I would never give it away. It was time to pay him back. I needed to face my fear that I'd find him murdered. Push any thoughts that he'd been harmed out of my brain and help him. I'd figure the rest out as I went. Right, time to pull up my big-girl panties and go.

I put my black beanie on and slipped the camera strap over my head—I was a butterfingers, and there was no way I wanted to drop my baby—and stepped out into the cold. The cloudy sky was more white fluff than heavy grey, and a gentle breeze had started, although "gentle" didn't aptly convey the chill it created. Brrr. I should have worn my ski jacket too.

The village green was to my left, but I turned right and headed towards the town centre and the pretty Tudor shops I'd noticed on our drive in. Maybe starting with architecture photos would be fun—at least the buildings couldn't die. As I walked, I removed the lens cap and put it in my jeans pocket. I turned the camera on and chose the setting I wanted—I'd start with automatic settings then move to manual when I had an idea of the effect I wanted. Part of what I loved was the experimental aspect. I could try different things, and if it didn't work, so what. Sometimes I lucked out on the most incredible shots, although James said it wasn't luck. I quirked one side of my mouth up in a half smile. I *was* going to see him again, and he would be alive and well.

There they were, across the road. The footpath was

narrow, so I'd take some shots from this side of the street and move to the other for a different angle later. I'd start with a wider angle and change focus as I went. I framed one terrace containing two shops into the first shot, leaving a touch of grey sky above the chimneys and the whole of the paved footpath in front. A large, shiny black door sat in the centre, which gave access to flats above, and each shop had their own front door—one angled on either side of the bigger door. The shop on the right was an interior design shop. The window display comprised a gorgeous two-seater sofa with fawn-striped fabric. Above it and to the sides hung different chandeliers, all giving off a welcoming yellow glow. I wanted to live in that shop. If I were rich, I'd totally hire an interior designer. My brief would be elegant yet comfortable, a mixture of antique and hotel. *Dream on, Lily.*

A chill prickled the back of my neck. I shuddered and turned around. Nope, no one was watching me, at least not that I could see. I'd had a sense of being followed just before I reached Costa's as well but chalked it down to Millicent and Angelica's repeated warnings to be careful. They'd made me paranoid. I shook my head and turned back around. It was time to get busy with my camera. I grinned. This was it: I was actually standing in a quaint English village and taking photos.

I'd taken about five shots when I noticed a woman in the second-floor dormer window. It was a large dormer, housing a row of five tall, white-painted timber panes. She stared straight at me, and she was solid, but she was dressed in a scoop-necked dress with lace sleeves and a tapered waist going to a full skirt. Unless someone was having a dress-up party, that was pretty weird. It looked like a dress from about two hundred years ago. I clicked twice, and then she disappeared.

My heart raced. Was I seeing the past or a ghost? I kept looking through the viewfinder, but she didn't reappear. I lowered the camera and looked back at my shots, and sure enough, there she was and then she wasn't. I zoomed in on the screen to get a better look, and yep, she was wearing an antique dress. Okay, I could test my theory by asking the shop owner if there was any type of re-enactment or dress-ups going on.

There was a fair amount of traffic zipping both ways. Once there was a break, I dashed across the road and to the left-hand shop—a wine bar. My friends would love this. The timber floor creaked, announcing my entry. Dimly lit and with exposed timber ceiling beams, it had a relaxed and old-world vibe. A young woman in a white shirt stood behind the bar. "Afternoon. What will it be, luv?" Her accent wasn't as refined as Angelica's, but it was still super British and therefore awesome.

"I'm not actually in here to drink. I hope that's okay. I wanted to ask a question."

"Ask away! Are you Australian?"

"I sure am. I'm over here visiting my brother."

"Wonderful. I 'ave a friend in Brisbane. 'er name's Patricia. Do you know her?"

I bit my lip. Was she having me on? The expectant expression on her face told me otherwise. "No, sorry. I'm from Sydney, which is a long way south of there. I don't know any Patricias, actually."

Her face fell. "Oh, no matter. Wha' can I 'elp you with, then?"

"Are there any events around here today where people are dressing in olden-day clothes? I thought I saw a woman standing at the window upstairs wearing a gorgeous dress."

Her brows drew close together as she thought. "I can't say there is, luv. Was this the first or second floor?"

"The second floor."

"Those tenants are away this week. They're not back for another few days. They didn't tell me they had anyone mindin' the place. Thanks for lettin' me know. I'll go up later and check nothin' untoward is goin' on."

"Thanks. And you have a beautiful bar. I'll have to bring my brother one night." Because we were going to find him.

"You do that, luv. And enjoy your stay."

"Thanks." I smiled and walked back out to the street. That didn't solve anything. There may or may not be someone up there. Gah! Why couldn't things be easy? I lifted my camera and watched the street through its filter. I took a few close-ups of the shop front, concentrating on the black window frame and part of the interior design display. Then I walked up the street, looking through my camera, waiting for anything else unusual to pop up.

I heard a car slow behind me, which was odd, because there wasn't enough room to park on the side of the street. I turned. A black van had mounted the footpath right behind me. Before it had even stopped, a man wearing a black balaclava jumped out of the passenger side and ran at me.

Maybe he was going to run past me and I was going to be majorly embarrassed, but there was no one else near me, and why run when someone was already driving you? Plus the whole balaclava thing kind of said, "I'm a criminal. Fear me." My pulse thundered in my ears, and I took off, sprinting.

I willed my legs to move faster past the shop fronts and sucked air into my lungs, ignoring the burn in my quads. My shoes slapped on the brick paving. I clutched my camera to my chest so it wouldn't bounce around. After about two hundred metres, there was a grunt and thud behind me. I risked a look over my shoulder.

A blond monster of a man—his arms were huge—was on top of the bad guy, pounding into him with his fists, but no one was chasing me now. The driver of the black van got out. *Oh no*! He stalked towards the fight, fists clenched. He had a stocking over his head, which squished his nose against his face, but his grimace was clear.

I drew in much-needed air and tried to catch my breath. How could I help the man who had come to my aid? I couldn't just stand here and wait for something bad to happen to him.

Stocking-face guy had almost reached the fight.

Heart racing, I walked back towards the men, shooting photos as I went. At least I'd have evidence for the police if they needed it. I made sure to include the black van. I stopped shooting. Across the road, people had stopped to watch, but no one ran over to help. Cowards, although, to be fair, those were three big men.

Stocking-face grabbed the blond guy by the back of his jacket, near his neck, and tried to yank him off the other guy. Someone grunted. I looked around for a weapon, anything I could bash stocking-face on the head with. There was nothing. The only hard thing I had was my camera, and there was no way I was using that.

Stuff it. I was going in anyway. The martial arts Dad made me do from ten to fourteen had to count for something—if only I could remember it.

Stocking-face had managed to get the blond guy off his accomplice, and I winced. *Please don't hurt him.*

Another car pulled up behind the van. Stocking-face yelled something to his friend, punched the blond guy in the face and ran for his van. *Crap, that had to have hurt!* Balaclava-guy stood awkwardly and limped-ran to the van and got in.

I sprinted, reaching the blond guy just as they started to drive. The van sped towards us. I pulled my saviour to the side, jamming us against the wall. Jeepers! I was breathing hard as adrenaline coursed through my body.

The arseholes steered back to the road, tyres screeching, and sped away.

A deep voice said, "I leave you alone for five minutes, and this is what happens."

I turned. Another man, the driver of the other car, I assumed, had his hand on the blond guy's shoulder, checking out the massive purpling eye that was already swelling shut. Both men towered over my five-foot-seven-self. They must have been six three, even six four. The new guy turned his blue-grey eyes on me. His stern expression reminded me of Angelica's. "Are you okay?"

I stared. My cheeks heated, and butterflies swarmed from my stomach into my chest. If my heart hadn't already been racing from the violence, it would have just started. Even through my shock and his cranky demeanour, I couldn't ignore the way this man affected me. All rational thought fled. Those light-coloured eyes set against his dark hair, and what about that defined jaw? No man should be this good looking. It wasn't fair to make the rest of us feel so inferior and tongue-tied. He was most likely used to women falling at his feet and was probably secretly wishing he didn't have to deal with me.

He stared at me, waiting for an answer. *Oh, right.* I nodded, because the brain-to-mouth connection hadn't yet resumed.

"Are you sure you're okay?" Giving up on me, he turned to his friend. "She didn't get hit, did she?"

"No, man. She wasn't near the fight. She's fast. That guy couldn't catch her, not even close."

"Cool." That stormy gaze was back on me. *Gulp.* "So, you're okay?"

I cleared my throat and tried not to sound like I thought he was the most gorgeous man I'd ever seen. *Casual, Lily. You can do it.* "Yeah, I'm good, thanks." I turned to the blond guy. "Thanks so much for helping me. I have no idea what just happened, but I think that guy really was going to grab me. I didn't realise it was so dangerous around here."

He gazed at me out of his one good eye, which happened to be a nice shade of hazel. What are the odds of meeting two hot men at once? This would be one to text the girls about. "It's not, usually. I saw them pull over. Lucky I was here, aye." He tried to grin, but it turned into a wince as the movement must have hurt his eye.

"I'm so sorry you got hurt. You took a big risk. If it hadn't been for you, who knows what would have happened. God knows, no one else was about to help." I looked across the road to the crowd still watching us. "Case in point." I shook my head. "Shouldn't we call the police? I took some photos, just in case we needed evidence."

The guys shared a knowing look, and Blondie said, "We're actually detectives. Just going down the road for lunch. That's why I helped. I'm trained to do this stuff. We can file a report."

"Shouldn't I provide a statement?"

Mr tall, dark, and broody jumped in. "That won't be necessary for now. We have it under control. I need to get this guy back to the station and get ice on his ugly mug. You can give us your number, and if we need anything, we'll give you a call."

"Okay, but I have an Australian number. I'll need to activate roaming. It should be working by tomorrow."

Grey eyes pulled out his phone. "Shoot."

"My name's Lily Bianchi and my number's +61416344988."

He punched the information in then gave a curt nod. "Are you staying near here?"

"Yes, just down there." I pointed. My street wasn't that far from where I'd ended up.

He looked at me like he was my angry father rather than a guy not much older than me. "Maybe go straight home, just in case they come back." I was shaken, and admittedly, concerned they might return, but I didn't want my adventure to be over, and damned if I didn't want the criminals to win by scaring me into hiding. I still had things to check out. He must've seen the expression on my face. "Promise me you'll go home. It's just for one afternoon." He narrowed his eyes.

I huffed out a breath and rolled my eyes. Not my most mature moment ever, but I had things to do, and his bossiness made me want to rebel. I didn't have time to be locked up all afternoon. I had magic to explore so I could hopefully save my brother. His narrowed gaze squinted further.

"All right, all right, don't strain your face. I'll go home right now."

He smirked. "Good. Now stay safe, Lily."

I gave him my crankiest face then turned and smiled at Blondie. "Thanks again."

Blondie gave me a careful smile. "Anytime."

They got into their car as I crossed the road and headed home. What the hell had just happened? And what were the odds of a policeman passing by right when you needed one? Maybe there were more per capita over here. Were they really police? Oh my God, what if I'd just given my number to some crazy psychos, but then, why would they have helped me if they weren't detectives? My head hurt.

As I walked down our narrow tree-lined street, I intermittently looked over my shoulder. I wouldn't be taken by surprise again. What just happened was crazy. True, crazy had become my life, apparently. Nothing like that had ever happened to me in twenty-four years in Sydney. I hadn't even been here for twenty-four hours. And what was I going to tell Millicent and Angelica? If they heard about this, they'd never let me go for a walk alone again, and I valued my solitary time. But if I didn't tell them and they found out later, there'd be hell to pay. Even if there was some connection between James being kidnapped and what just happened, which I refused to believe, I needed to be the person who made decisions about where I went and what I did. I sighed. I didn't want to live my life in fear.

With one last check to make sure I hadn't been followed, I turned into our driveway and stopped to take a deep breath and just *be*. So much had happened in a short time that I needed to figure out where I was at. I shut my eyes and relished the cold air filling my nose and lungs. What could I smell? Damp earth and magnolia blooms. What could I hear? Distant cars, a jumbo jet, and a dog barking next door. I opened my eyes. The gravel drive was just as pretty as when we arrived, with blooming magnolia trees lining one side and a low box hedge the other. Behind the magnolias was a head-high brick boundary fence, the textured brick peeking out from under the dark green leaves of a jasmine vine. It wasn't flowering, but it was still pretty.

I flicked the camera switch to on and snapped shots of the garden, showing the lines of the trees and wall. The

close-ups of the magnolia flowers filled my lens with stunning pink tones fading to white. Wow, a ladybug was sitting
on the outside of a petal. *Click, click, click.* I moved further
down the drive and aimed my camera at the house, but
before I could snap anything, Millicent came running out.

"Lily, are you okay?"

She couldn't know, could she? I thought she could only
read animal minds. Also, I wasn't transmitting right now,
was I? I checked, and my blue bubble was still there. "Ah,
yeah, but I do have something to tell you. Why don't we go
inside?"

Her eyes widened. "I knew something had happened. I
could feel it. I'm tuned into the feelings of those
around me."

Oh God, not another secret power I'd have to watch out
for. "Like an empath, but better?"

"Yes, just like that. I sensed great stress and panic."

"Just for the record, there was no panicking. I was calm
the whole time, at least I think I was." We'd reached the
living area, and I sat on the Chesterfield. "When I was out,
this man tried to grab me. I got away and then some other
guy came and beat him up." The abbreviated version would
have to do. I didn't want this to get blown out of proportion.

"What?!" she shrieked. Her face paled, as if that were
even possible.

But then I realised she'd already been through all of this.
"Hey, I'm okay. Sorry. I don't want you to freak out on my
account. Honestly, I'm fine. It was random, just wrong
place, wrong time. You know?"

"You really think it was random?" Millicent looked so innocent and was normally softly spoken, so her shrewd assessment was unexpected.

She definitely made a good point, one I had considered briefly but didn't want to think about. What were the odds that two siblings would get randomly kidnapped within one week—probably worse than a policeman showing up at the right time?

Crap. Now I couldn't ignore the small voice that said someone might be after me too.

"I'm calling Angelica." Millicent walked to a semi-circular table sitting under the window. An old-fashioned green phone sat on it. She picked up the receiver and dialled by sticking her index finger into the different circles one at a time and spinning the dial around. Why wouldn't she just use a mobile? "Angelica, we have a problem." She stared out the window, leaning forward so her face was almost pressed against the glass. Was she looking for bad guys? "Lily was almost kidnapped. She says a policeman just happened to be there at the right time, and he saved her… yes. Yes, I know." She straightened and turned to look at me. "Okay, fine. We'll be here. See you soon." She hung up.

I hated being the subject of a conversation I couldn't hear. "So, what's happening?"

"Angelica is sending the car. It should be here shortly. We're going to headquarters. She doesn't want you out of her sight."

Ah, crap. This wasn't even my fault, and it was like I was being punished. Yes, she wanted to keep me safe, but I still couldn't be happy about it. Headquarters was probably some kind of bunker, like they showed on TV. But I knew there'd be no point arguing. Stuff it. I'd make the most of my time by editing some of Tracy's photos while I was there. "I'm just going to grab my laptop. Be right back."

"Okay." She was back to staring out the window, her shoulders drooping, and her voice sounding down. Gah, I was supposed to be all out of cuddles, but she looked so sad. I went and wrapped my arms around her.

"It'll be okay. We'll find James. You'll see."

She sniffed and nodded. "I'll be okay." She stood straight. Her eyes were glassy with unshed tears. "Go get your stuff. He'll be here soon."

I ducked to the toilet, because who knew how far it was to the Bureau's headquarters. By the time I grabbed my laptop and returned downstairs, the driver, a middle-aged man wearing a dark suit and dark cap, was standing in the vestibule. Millicent walked past me on her way to the front door. "Let's go."

I followed her, and the driver came next, locking the door behind him. He rushed to open the car door for us. I climbed into the back first, so Millicent didn't have to climb across the seat. I knew deep down that she was strong, but this afternoon, she appeared fragile, and I didn't want to make anything harder for her. Not that climbing across a back seat was an Olympic event, but you know.

We drove west for around twenty-five minutes before turning down another narrow road. A high brick wall with barbwire on the top ran parallel to the road. Partway along, we pulled into a driveway that stopped at wrought-iron gates. The sign posted on the wall proclaimed *Vision Industries Pty Ltd*. About thirty metres behind the gates was a compact shed with a small window, and a camera mounted on the roof. Security.

Our driver pulled a two-way, walkie-talkie thing from his front seat and spoke into it. "It's Jones. We're here."

The gates clicked then slowly opened inwards. A guard came out of his little shed and waved as we went past. Jones waved back. We continued to a massive white concrete and glass two-storey building that looked more like a science lab than anything else. Vision Industries must be a front, unless PIB was renting space from them?

"Is this where you and James work?"

She turned to me. "Yes. It's also where we met." Her small smile was like a glimpse of sun on a cloudy day.

"I remember him calling to tell me he'd met the love of his life. He was always vague about work, but he couldn't stop talking about you." They were so great together: they loved animals, spicy food, hiking, and their jobs, and they were both witches. All I knew was that James, for the most part, had been ridiculously happy since he'd met Millicent, and she'd been nothing but kind to me, even if it was via long distance.

Jones opened the car door for Millicent, and I let myself out my own door. Patience was not one of my virtues. Millicent walked around to my side of the car and to the wide glass entry doors. Security personnel guarded the doors—one machine-gun toting muscleman on each side. Why did they need guns if everyone had magic? Maybe you had to shoot people who were stronger magically than you. Interesting.

Millicent's court shoes clicked on the polished concrete floor as she made her way to a security checkpoint. We had to place anything metal on a table and walk through an airport-style scanner. My sister-in-law pulled a handgun from a holster under her arm before going through. Wow, since when was she armed? I tried to hide my surprise. I only had my harmless laptop, phone, and camera to put on the table. I felt like I didn't fit in, and we hadn't even cleared security. I was the protectee, not the protector. That didn't sit well with me. I hated relying on anyone else. It conjured feelings of guilt and inadequacy. Maybe I should see a therapist when I got home.

Once we made it through there, minus Jones, we were signed in at a glowing white counter. Everything was alabaster and shiny, except for the dark-tinted windows at the front of the building. Millicent and I were then handed off to an older man in a black suit and tie. He had the body and stature of someone much younger, but his grey hair was thinning at the temples, and deep lines creased his brow. He wore an earpiece, like the secret service guys on TV. Millicent introduced us. "Hi, Gus. This is my sister-in-law, Lily."

I smiled and held out my hand. "Pleased to meet you, Gus."

He shook my hand. "The pleasure is all mine. Your brother's a hell of a guy."

"Thank you."

"I'm your liaison while you're here. Anything you need, just ask. I'll try and stay in the background as much as possible, but I'm never too far away."

"Thanks." *I think.* I'm sure that was code for "We're always watching."

Gus used his security tag to get us through one door, one corridor, a lift to the first floor, then another heavy door followed by another corridor. The people we passed were either dressed in black suits, white shirts, and black ties—the uniform designer here must have loved *Men in Black*—or they wore street clothes—jeans, jumpers, and T-shirts. A few waved to Gus or said hello, and a couple had liaison-looking people following them.

We turned a few corners until I had no idea which way was north and which way south. Millicent and Gus chatted the whole time. I found out Gus's wife had just had her gallbladder removed but was doing well, he had successfully cooked a beef stew in her absence, and his dog had vomited on the rug this morning. Ew. We came to a door marked M3 and stopped. Gus swiped, and the door lock clicked.

Millicent turned to me. "Can you just wait out here with Gus for a few minutes? There's a meeting taking place, and I'm not sure when Angelica wants you to come in."

"Not a prob."

Gus held the door open for her then shut it as soon as she entered. I didn't see much, except that the walls were pale blue rather than white. So, what now? Gus folded his arms and alternated between staring down the corridor and staring at his shoes. There were no chairs out here, no TV, nothing to do except stand awkwardly and notice how awkward Gus was now that Millicent had gone and left two apparent introverts together. I thought of trying to start a conversation, but then I realised how tired I was, and I didn't want to hear any more about dogs vomiting.

What time was it? I checked my phone. 2:00 p.m. That meant it was 11:00 p.m. at home. Close to my bedtime. I yawned. Stuff decorum. I leaned against the wall and slid to the floor. It was cold on my backside, but I was beyond caring. I was about to check Facebook when I remembered I had no roaming set up, so it would have cost a small fortune. *Grrr.* I could start editing, but what if I was called into the meeting. Then I'd have to shut down the laptop quickly—it wasn't safe to carry it while it was on. You could wreck the hard drive, and I loved my laptop almost as much as my camera. I was such a sucker for technology.

I wondered what they were discussing in there—if it was random or James related. Tears burnt my eyes. What if he were dead? Or what if he were alive but badly hurt and being tortured? Considering his line of work, that was a distinct possibility. How could I help find him? Hopelessness washed over me, just like when I was fourteen. I hung my head and hugged my knees. My parents went missing while they were over here. Were they targeted because they used to work at the Bureau? The police reported they had just disappeared, but there were no suspicious circumstances— except the fact they actually disappeared. Had the Bureau tried to find them? And if they had, did they have a file I could look at? My heart hurt whenever I thought about my parents. Not knowing what happened left a gaping wound. Were they dead or living as prisoners somewhere? I could never believe they had willingly walked away from my brother and me. But if they were dead, how did they die? Were their last few minutes filled with pain and terror, or had it been quick? Where were their bodies? I thought of them every day, and I knew that would never change. James and I hadn't had a day of peace, not really, since it had happened. Now I was reliving that nightmare all over again.

"Lily?"

I jumped. *Jesus!* Millicent had snuck out and was standing next to me. Maybe she hadn't snuck. I'd kind of been in my own world.

"They're ready to see you."

I stood and followed her through the door, curious as to who the "we" would be, and why they wanted to meet me. I still didn't see how I could help.

Sitting around an eight-seat oval table were Angelica, a young woman in a stylish black suit jacket and mint-green shirt, her blonde hair up in a French roll who managed to make her reading glasses look sexy, a man in his forties with thick, wavy dark hair, and a thin man in his fifties, whose grey hair was pulled back in a low ponytail. His thick grey beard was neatly trimmed, and even though his white shirt only had one top button undone, his chest hair still managed to sneak out, and he wore a silver bracelet on one wrist.

They stared at me, not even trying to hide their assessing gazes. I was sure Angelica had already made her judgement, but she probably saw how I reacted to this situation. They supposedly wanted me here to help, but where were the friendly smiles and comments welcoming me to England? What about a little sympathy and enquiries as to how I was holding up, considering my brother was missing? Cold-hearted witches.

The guy with the mauve tie—the dark-haired one—had a cocky confidence, and he sat at the head of the table, so he was probably the boss. I narrowed my eyes ever so slightly and let my anger slide to the surface. I walked to his seat and looked down at him, meeting his calculating stare with a you-can-stick-your-opinion-up-your-you-know-what-you-heartless-bastard stare. I owed these people nothing, and so far, they hadn't done anything to help me or my brother. He was still missing, and I was twenty-four hours from home with no one who really cared, except for Millicent, but she had her own crap to deal with. My anger had been building since yesterday, and I had only just realised it. It took a lot to piss me off, and I hated to say, they'd gotten me there.

He steepled his fingers. "She has got some spunk, Angelica. My word, what a good find." What the? What was I: a showjumping horse or an antiquity? I levelled my stare at Angelica, and she gave it right back, with interest. How could she sell me out so quickly? Had this meeting just been a table of people dissecting James's sister? What were they sizing me up for? I didn't think I wanted to know. If it weren't for a chance at finding James, I would have turned, left, and not stopped until I was on a plane home.

The modelesque woman stood and walked around the table. She offered her right hand. "I'm Snezana. Pleased to meet you, Lily." I hesitated to shake her hand, but then she smiled, and I felt guilty, so I followed the niceties. "Why don't you come and sit next to me. We were just discussing a new lead on the case and were hoping you could help."

I let her lead me to the seat next to hers. "Would you like a glass of water or a coffee?" Gee, she really was nice. *Bad Lily.*

"Nothing, but thanks anyway." I hated being a bother.

Millicent sat across from me but wouldn't meet my gaze. I couldn't blame her. If I could shoot lasers from my eyes, there'd be two dead people already. I'd have to find out if that was a viable witch skill.

The guy at the head of the table straightened his already straight tie—hmm, had I rattled him just a little? Nice. "Now that Lily's here, we can do the rest of the introductions." His accent was as posh as they came. He spoke just loud enough to give his words gravity while not appearing to be trying too hard. I actually had to lean forward to hear him—everyone did. We looked ridiculous, like we were waiting on him to reveal what happens after you die, or the spell for the laser death glare. I could almost guarantee he was doing it on purpose. Jerk. "As you've just learned, that's Snezana. She's James's assistant and the lead coordinator on this case. You obviously know Angelica, our head of operations, and Millicent, one of our top investigators, and then there's Timothy, head of IT, and James's direct report"— Timothy gave me a sad smile, so he was probably one of the good ones. Three out of five was actually pretty good. "And I'm the big boss around here. Drake Pembleton the Third.

Despite how it seems, we're happy to have you here, and I can assure you, we're doing all we can to get your brother back, including asking for your help. We pride ourselves on a job well done at PIB. I'll let Snezana take it from here." He leaned back and folded his hands across his slightly rounded tummy.

I turned my chair towards Snezana. She gave me a reassuring smile. "Let me know if you're okay as we go, okay, Lily? I'm going to be asking a few questions that might be upsetting." I nodded. "Good. I understand you were set upon by two men today. Could you tell us what happened, and please leave nothing out? We need to know everything you can remember."

How had they heard about that already? It couldn't have been from Millicent, because I told her one guy tried to jump me. "I'd just come out of the wine bar in the main street...."

Angelica raised her brows then shook her head. "Drinking so early, Lily?"

"What? No! I'll explain later. It's not important right now. So, I came out of the wine bar and turned right. As I walked farther up the street, I heard a vehicle slow down behind me. I knew there was nowhere to park, so I looked around. A black van mounted the footpath and drove right behind me before it stopped and a guy jumped out."

"What did he look like?"

"He was tall, about six foot one. He had a balaclava over his face and was wearing blue jeans and maybe a jumper. I can't remember." I furrowed my brow. What colour was his top? Surely I could remember—it had only happened this afternoon. *Come on, brain, think.* "Whatever his top was, he had long sleeves and it was some kind of lighter colour, like a light-brown or fawn."

"They're the same colour, dear."

Why did Angelica hate me so much?

"Yeah, right, well, that must be the colour it was, then."

Snezana leaned over and patted my arm. "It's okay. Memory isn't as reliable as you think, but there might be something you do remember quite clearly that gives us a breakthrough." Should I mention the photos I'd taken? No, then they'd confiscate my camera and might find out about my special skill, if that's what it was.

I described the rest of what I remembered and ended with, "Then another guy with dark straight hair, Blondie's friend, came along, and the bad guys ran back to their van and drove off. The guys who helped me said they were police. Were they?"

A few beats of silence met my question. Snezana cleared her throat and continued. "We'll discuss that later. For now, do you remember anything about the man who tried to attack you? Did he have any tattoos, scars?"

"I couldn't see any of him. Clothes covered him from head to toe. I didn't get close enough to get a good look at his hands. Sorry."

"And are you sure he was after you? Do you think he could have been maybe going to rob a shop?"

"I suppose he could have been. I wasn't totally sure, but it looked like he was running for me, but he didn't say anything, and I couldn't see his eyes, so, maybe." But I know how I'd felt: targeted, scared. Could I have gotten it wrong?

"Thank you, Lily. We appreciate your time."

So that was it? They asked me here to discredit my version of events, so they could file it and move on, put it down to a witch at the wrong place, wrong time. I sighed. Whatever. "Before I go, you said you had a breakthrough on my brother's case. What was it?"

Snezana looked to the big boss. He gave an almost imperceptible shake of his head. James's assistant gave me her attention again. "We can't say at this stage, I'm afraid. If you'd had some other information about the attackers, we would have had something to discuss, but now we can't. I'm so sorry." She included Millicent in her apology.

My poor sister-in-law nodded and stood quickly. "You'll have to excuse me." She hurried out of the room, probably trying to beat her tears. I couldn't imagine she wanted to cry in front of her colleagues, especially ones as cold-hearted as these.

Snezana shared another serious look with Drake Pembleton the Third, but I couldn't get what that was about. Whatever it was, it seemed like some kind of negative comment about Millicent. Arsehats.

I stood. "Please excuse me." I followed her out. I was epically failing to find my brother at that moment, but there was still someone I could help.

I caught up with Millicent but didn't say anything. We walked side by side, Gus silently following behind, until we'd almost reached the end of the hallway, where we stopped in front of a closed office door. She hovered her hand over the door handle and mumbled a few words. The lock clicked, and the door swung open. *Ooh, magic.*

"I'll just be out here, then," Gus said.

"Thanks, Gus." Millicent led me into her office suite and shut the door behind us. She went through a functional reception area, which had a receptionist's desk—currently vacant—a large plastic fern against one wall, and two two-seater sky-blue sofas. She continued into another room, walked around a large mahogany table and sat in a plush, leather, high-backed office chair. "Sit down, Lily. I just need to gather my thoughts for a minute."

"Yeah, sure." I sat in one of two sixties-inspired black fabric chairs and put my camera and laptop bag on her table. Three framed university degrees hung on her wall— smart lady. A coat rack stood in the corner next to a mini-fridge and black filing cabinet. Her uncluttered desk held an office phone, a pink penholder, a three-tiered desk organiser, and two framed photos. I turned them around. One was of her and James's dogs, two adorable Labradors, one yellow and one black. I picked up the other photo to get a closer look.

James and Millicent, from the shoulders up, cheeks rosy and hair windblown, stood in front of a gorgeous view that could just be seen over their shoulders, indicating they were on a hilltop somewhere. Their smiles were so wide that I could almost see the gap where one of James's top molars had been. He'd been smashed in the face at hockey when he was thirteen. What if I never saw him again? Damn stupid tears burning my eyes. I blinked and bit my tongue. I would not cry. Millicent needed me to be strong.

I placed the photo back on the table. "What are we going to do, Mill?"

"I'm not sure, but something needs to happen soon, or we'll never get him back." She clenched her jaw, and her eyes glistened with the tears she was trying not to shed. She took a deep breath, attempting to compose herself. "Did you get any good photos before the drama this afternoon?" We both needed a change of subject.

"I think so. There are the cutest Tudor buildings in Westerham. I'm kind of pissed that my visit was cut short. Especially since I was apparently overreacting." I rolled my eyes. That reminded me of the woman in the window. Hmm. "Millicent, I might have an idea, but I want to take some photos first." If I could trust anyone in this place, it was my sister-in-law. "Can I take a few shots in here?"

"That should be fine, as long as you delete them before you leave. This is a high-security facility. I'm surprised they let you in with that camera."

"Oh, okay." I'm glad they hadn't tried to confiscate it. They may have had to arrest me.

I grabbed my Nikon, undid the lens cap, and flicked the On switch. I walked out to the reception area and pointed the camera at the receptionist's desk. Nothing. It all looked as it had before. I swivelled around slowly, taking everything in through the viewfinder. Nothing. Looked like my hunch was wrong, but I'd try in Millicent's office, just in case.

I kept looking through the camera as I entered Millicent's office. Millicent sat in the same spot—nothing unusual there. I joined her behind her desk and pointed my camera at the guest chairs. Maybe I needed to try harder? I took a couple of deep breaths and shut everything else out. Concentrating all my thoughts to capturing the best shot, I started shooting. *Click. Click. Click. Click.* There! Oh my God! I clicked a few more frames. This was awesome! I was so excited; I wanted to scream. I stomped my feet a few times in a happy dance.

"Eeek! Look at this." I pressed the Play button to bring up the images I'd just taken, and I passed the camera to Millicent. "Look at that."

Her confused expression turned to wonder, her mouth dropping open as she gazed at the screen. Then she blushed. Standing behind the chairs, in another time, were James and Millicent, locked in a passionate kiss. I chuckled. "You two are so cute together."

She bit her lip, and when she looked at me, a tear tracked down her cheek. For the first time since I'd arrived, hope shone from her gaze. But she placed her pointer finger in front of her mouth in a shushing gesture. I looked around. Of course the place would be bugged, probably by witchy means at the very least. Thank goodness I hadn't explained my theory.

She stood. "What do you say we take a drive, go find

some coffee? Being here reminds me of James. Today's not been a great day."

"Yeah, why not. You know I'm always up for a coffee." I smiled. I hoped Millicent was going to take me for a drive to the place James disappeared from.

A knock came from the main door. We both looked there and back at each other. Please don't be Angelica. She hadn't stood up for either of us in the meeting. Whatever her agenda was, I was sure I wouldn't like it.

Millicent went and opened the door, then returned, a scowl on her face that quickly changed to neutral. Strange. Snezana followed her in. "Hi, ladies. I just wanted to come in here and say sorry about what happened in the meeting. I wish I had better news to tell you. I was hoping you might want to go to the cafeteria and grab some coffee." Suspicious much, or was I just being paranoid again?

"Um..." I looked to Millicent for direction.

"You two go. I have a couple of reports to look over. We can catch a ride home with Angelica later, Lily."

"But—"

Her smile was bright, forced. "No, go. I'm not great company at the moment anyway."

"Are you sure you'll be okay?" What had just happened? Something was definitely going on between Millicent and Snezana.

"I've survived a week so far. I'm sure I'll be good for one more afternoon."

I grabbed my phone, more out of habit than anything,

but maybe I could try taking some photos with it later. See what happened. "All right, but I won't be long. Bye."

"Bye, Millicent. Don't work too hard," Snezana threw over her shoulder. It was subtle, and I didn't know the woman, so I couldn't be sure if she was being a bitch or not. I'd have to tread carefully with this one. But being James's secretary, maybe she had some information on who could have done this, if it was work related.

The woman chatted the whole way down the corridor, into the lift, and along another corridor until we walked through double doors to a large cafeteria. Apparently she'd worked here for about one year, had two older brothers, and a mother who everyone kept mistaking for her sister, because she looked so young.

There weren't a lot of people in here since it was mid-afternoon, but still, knives, forks, and cups clinked and echoed in the concrete chamber. It was a self-service arrangement with a row of hot food under glass, and a cabinet of cakes. The food looked good. My stomach grumbled at the smell of green chicken curry and beef stroganoff, but then the cheesecake and black forest cake also looked delish. I didn't have room for all of it, though, so a difficult decision had to be made.

"Have whatever you like. It's free. Part of the perks of working for the government."

"But I don't work here. Are you sure it's still free?"

"You're my guest." She smiled. "I've been dying to meet James's little sister. He's always talking about you and your job as a photographer. It sounds so cool. He mentioned you were trying to put together some shots to have an exhibition." She led us to a table and sat.

"I was, but work was a bit busy, so I haven't done anything about it for a while. I'd love to have an exhibition and sell my creative work. Weddings are okay, and I appreciate I get to do what I love for a living, but a lot of time I'm sacrificing my creativity to get the quintessential wedding shots. And, people can be such a pain to deal with. You should try getting a bride, ten bridesmaids, plus two page girls looking at the camera and smiling simultaneously. And someone always blinks at the wrong time. I prefer having my iPod on and wandering around by myself. Just me, some good music, and my camera." I shrugged. "I'm going to grab a coffee and some cake. Do you want anything?"

"No, thank you. I'm good. I had lunch three hours ago." Three hours was a long time between meals in my world. But I guessed being skinny meant not eating. She was welcome to her hunger.

"I'll be back in a minute." I grabbed a cappuccino and a cheesecake then returned to Snezana. She gazed at me with a serene smile on her face, which was a little bit creepy. To hide my discomfort, I focussed on setting my food up on the table. "What's it like to work for my brother? He was always so organised and bossy at home. My messes used to do his head in." I glanced up, and her expression was normal again. Thank God.

"Ha, yes, he's very tidy, but that's a commendable trait in a man... or woman, or anyone really." *Okaaay.* "He's actually really nice to work for. He expects things to be done properly, but he's nice if you make a mistake. I couldn't imagine working for anyone else now. We get along so well too. Did he ever mention me?"

That was a weird question. "No, but then, I didn't even know he worked here, or that he was a witch, or that witches even existed, so I wouldn't take it personally. Did he have any enemies at work? I just can't imagine who'd want to hurt him." I knew she would have passed on any information that was important to people who knew what they were doing, but I couldn't help asking.

"Another guy in his division, Anthony, is very competitive. He hates that James is smarter than him and that James was promoted before him, even though your brother's younger. I told Angelica—she's heading this investigation. I have no idea if she looked into it." She bit her bottom lip and looked to be considering something before she spoke. "Can I ask you a personal question?"

I swallowed a gulp of coffee. "Sure."

"Are you and Millicent close?"

I shrugged. "A little. I mean, I like her and we get along well, but we haven't spent much time together in person since we live in different countries, but we Skype a lot. The fact James loves her is a big endorsement as to her character too." I smiled.

She looked at my phone. "Is that the iPhone 8?"

"Yep. I updated my plan a couple of months ago and got this. The X was a bit pricey."

"Can I have a look?"

"Sure." I handed it over. "I love Apple stuff."

She grinned. "Me too." She turned the phone over, weighed it in her hand, and pressed the home button. "Good size. I was tossing up between this and the bigger version. This is a lot easier to handle." She mumbled something to herself then handed the phone back. "Thanks. I think I'll get one."

The phone gave me a small electric shock when I touched it. Bloody stupid power coming in. I hope I hadn't damaged the phone. I pressed the home button, relieved when it still worked.

A look crossed her face. Was that contemplation or worry?

"Well, I shouldn't be talking out of turn, and please don't repeat this. Actually, if I promise to tell you something, do you mind if I put a spell on you to make sure you can't repeat it?"

"You can do that?"

"Yes, but I need your permission. You can't put a spell like that on someone without their agreement. It's illegal. It's nothing more than a nondisclosure agreement, but witch style."

What if what she told me was something I decided had to be told? What if she told me who took my brother? Surely she couldn't know that. "I'm not sure. It's not who took my brother, is it?"

Snezana laughed. "Oh, my goodness, Lily, you're so funny!" Her voice softened and she looked at her lap. "If I knew who'd taken your brother, we would have him back by now." She sounded like someone who'd failed.

"Fair enough. I still have to ask, though: is it about something illegal? Because if it is, depending on what it was, I'd have to tell the police, so I can't agree to that."

She smiled and shook her head in a mood change that had my head spinning. "You're such a riot." Her fake laugh made me think she'd meant to say: you're such a pain in the behind. "No, it's nothing like that. Look, if you don't want to know, it's fine. It's probably nothing anyway, but it could have something to do with your brother's disappearance."

Could I trust her? Not really, but then James trusted her to be his assistant, to work closely with him and not spill any work secrets. And what if she told me something that made sense to no one else but me, something that helped find James? "Okay, but you can only tell me one thing under this agreement thing, and it can't be about something illegal." I wouldn't put it past her to make me an accessory to something. There was something about her I wasn't sure about. She had been fairly nice to me—the swan in a room full of vultures—but maybe she was only being nice because I was James's sister? I'd reserve my final judgement till later.

"Let's shake on it." We shook. Her hand was soft and warm, but her grip was hard—a reminder for me not to underestimate her. Although, maybe she'd make a good ally, especially if she had James's back. Gah, I was so confused.

"Give me your hands." We both leaned our arms over the table, our hands meeting in the middle. This time her grip was gentler. She looked into my eyes and said, "Repeat after me. I, Lily Katerina Bianchi…"

"I, Lily Katerina Bianchi…" How did she know my middle name?

"Will keep the following information in the strictest confidence…"

"Will keep the following information in the strictest confidence…"

"I will not repeat any part of this conversation to a living soul…"

"I will not repeat any part of this conversation to a living soul…"

"And if I do, I will die by choking."

What the freaking hell? "And if I do, I will die by choking." An electric charge shot up both my arms and lodged in my neck before fading away. What did I just agree to? I was clearly nuts.

Her smile was smug, like she had me where she wanted. *Please, can she only tell me some secret cookie recipe or something about Gus?* I wouldn't even care if it involved dog vomit.

"We're done." She released my hands but leaned closer and lowered her voice. "Millicent and James had a fight the day before he went missing. I know because they had it in his office in front of me. He threatened to leave her, and she said she'd never let that happen, that she would make him pay if he did."

This wasn't good. I wasn't Millicent's best friend, but I liked her, and I couldn't believe she'd ever threaten anyone, let alone the man she loved, but then again, I didn't know she was a gun-toting witch. "Why don't you want me to be able to tell anyone? You said you already told Angelica, right?"

"Yes, but I didn't want you spilling the beans to Millicent. If she were involved, you'd just give her a warning. Who knows, she might run, and we'll never find out what happened to James... assuming she's involved. He's such a handsome man. He could have had anyone. I have no idea why he picked that mousy bitch."

My eyes widened. Snezana's mouth worked itself into an *O*. Even she realised she'd gone too far. "I didn't mean it like that, but you have no idea the things James tells me. He's been miserable for months. Anyway, you can't repeat any of this, because you'll die."

I can't believe I agreed to this. "Can I ask her any questions without telling her anything."

"No, because if she suspects I said anything, my magic will know, and you'll die."

Crap. "What if I come back from here, don't say anything, and she wonders if you told me anything?"

"As long as you don't say, imply, write, or mention anything about our conversation, you should be okay, but I hadn't thought of that angle. You *should* be okay." She didn't look the least bit apologetic. What the hell had I gotten myself into? Now I had to avoid Millicent and she wouldn't know why, and we were supposed to take that drive.

I finished my coffee, but the second half of my cheesecake was a no-go zone. Who could eat when they were worried about choking to death? "How long does the spell last?"

"While I'm alive, it's valid, unless I undo it."

I'd never considered killing anyone before…. Ha ha, just kidding. Or was I? I laughed. *Good one, Lily.* Snezana stared at me, her eyes big and just a little fearful. I almost felt bad. "I'd never try and kill you. That's what you thought I was thinking. Isn't it?" Oh, but I had thought that, hadn't I. I wasn't serious. I was just having a joke with myself. Killing was bad, no matter the reason. *Yep.*

"Of course I didn't think that. Besides, I'm a strong witch. It would take a lot to kill me, and you're on your training wheels. You're quite harmless. James also said you were really nice. From what he says, you're not the killing kind."

"No, I guess not." Was it wrong that this disappointed me? "Thanks for the chat. I should get going. I have no idea when Angelica wants to leave, but thanks to you, I have to avoid Millicent."

"Don't do your nut, Lily. It's just business. Please don't hold this against me. I needed to tell you. Maybe you can find a way to out her, since you're family. You could get into her house."

"Wouldn't the police already have searched her house? And she's my sister-in-law. I can't believe she would do something like that."

"Yes, but I wonder if the police did a good job, since she's got the devastated wife role down pat, and she works here. I didn't peg you for someone who would let your brother down. Forget she's related to you by marriage. You owe it to your brother to do this. If you find anything, let me know. I'm the information coordinator on the case; don't forget. There's nothing more I want than to get James back. You have no idea how hard it's been to not have him here. We make such a great team. Who knows, maybe one day we'll be sisters-in-law. Wouldn't that be cool?"

No, no it wouldn't. Who says that about a married man who could possibly be dead? There was so much wrong with it that I didn't know how to answer and still be polite. I gave her my most awkward smile, jumped up and left. As I made my way to the lift, I realised I had no swipe card to get anywhere. Not only that, I needed to be alone and think about how I was going to handle the fact that if I believed Snezana, I couldn't trust Millicent, but if I trusted my instincts, I couldn't trust Snezana. Oh, and one wrong word, and I would die.

I turned to find my shadow. "Hey, Gus. Is there somewhere I can go to be by myself for a while? Preferably somewhere with a chair."

"Of course, Miss Lily. Inside or out?"

"Outside would be nice. I'm feeling a bit closed in. Can you do me a favour?"

"Of course."

"Can you get someone to bring me my camera and laptop from Millicent's office. I don't feel like going back there right now, and I need to get some work done."

"Not a problem." Gus placed his hand to his ear and put in my request to a guy named Frank, and then he swiped us into the lift.

Back on the ground floor, I signed out, and Gus showed me to an area to the right of the front doors. It was a small park with a smattering of mature trees. How did they get such green, perfect grass? In Sydney, half our grass was dead at any given time—a casualty of dry summers and scorching sun. An expanse of perfect lawn sloped gently down to a pond that had ducks, and oh my God! "Squirrels!" The little furry munchkins were skittering around the base of the nearest tree. As I approached, they raced up the trunk. I wanted to jump up and down and clap my hands, but I was wary of scaring them. If only I had some food to coax them down.

I looked up into the tree. "Hello, squirrels. How are you?" They were adorable, with their bushy tails and tiny paws. Ooh, look, one was cleaning its face. "You guys are so cute!"

Gus shook his head and laughed. "You Australians are so funny."

"Don't you think they're cute?"

He pulled a face. "No. They eat Pogo's food and make him bark. They're annoying vermin." Better the squirrels eat the food than the vomity dog. I didn't see a problem.

"You disappoint me, Gus. I thought you were one of the good ones."

He grinned. Finally, someone who got my humour. Maybe he wasn't so bad. "I am, miss, just not according to squirrels."

"Ha!" I smiled.

"There you are." Crap. I turned. Angelica stood there

holding my laptop bag and camera. "I heard you needed these."

I took them. "Thanks. I'll just be over at that bench working, if anyone needs me."

"Hang on a minute, please." Angelica turned to Gus. "Do you mind giving us a few minutes?"

"Not at all, ma'am." He turned and wandered back the way we came, although, I knew he wouldn't go too far. Goodness knew what I'd get up to if I was let loose around here. I was a right danger to society.

"Come, let's sit." We headed for the bench closest to the pond and sat. I watched the ducks glide happily around. Were there witch ducks? Oh, shit! I checked my brain barrier thing. Phew, it was still there. If I let my conversation with Snezana slip and Angelica read my mind, I'd die. Why hadn't I thought of that before? Oh, God, did I even remember the incantation? *These thoughts are mine; I do not wish to share. Protect them well, little bubble, something, something, something.* I was so dead.

"Angelica, do you mind repeating that mind-protection spell again? I've forgotten the bit at the end."

"Of course you have." Her tone was coated with disdain. "It's *These thoughts are mine; I do not wish to share. Protect them well, little bubble, with a barrier as invisible as air.*"

"Thank you. I should really write it down."

"Yes, you should."

We stared at the pond. While I wished she'd just say what she came to say and leave me in peace, I wasn't going to ask. Let her do the hard work for a change. I could out-silence the best of them: my second middle name was Awkward.

"A little bird told me someone took you for coffee."

"Yes. That coffee down there isn't half bad. The cheese-cake's nice too." As long as I kept the conversation away from anything to do with James, Millicent, or Snezana, I should be fine. I was up to the challenge.

"Did you learn anything you think could help?"

"Nope. But I do have a question. Is there a spell to block others from hearing us? I'm imagining there's a spell so people can hear what we're saying from far away. There must be a counter spell or a spell that can stop it in the first place."

"Someone's been thinking. It's about time."

"Seriously? I've been dumped into this crap with no warning, no experience, not to mention you've been rela-tively hostile the whole time. I think I'm doing freaking awesome."

"Awesomely."

"What?"

"It's awesomely, not awesome. Not that I'm trying to be difficult... well, not all the time. I do have a reputation to maintain, dear." She smiled, a real one. *Quick, someone erect a shrine that people could come and pray to—a miracle has occurred.* "The answer to your question is yes."

She moved her lips silently, probably to avoid being obvious about the fact she was casting this spell. She stood and walked the perimeter of our bench then sat again. "They're always listening: this *is* the Bureau, after all. It's full of police and spies answering to the government. What did you want to say?"

"I need to visit the place where James disappeared. Could we go there now?"

"We might be followed. It'll be easier for me to cloak our movements if we're leaving from home. Can you wait until tomorrow morning?"

"Okay."

"Are you going to tell me why you want to visit the field he was in when it happened? Our guys combed over it that day. I doubt there's any evidence left."

"I have a theory on how my magic works, but I don't know enough yet to tell you. I'd hate to get anyone's hopes up." I'd have to trust someone other than Millicent soon, because I couldn't ask Millicent to help—she had enough on her plate—and Angelica was the one who'd come to get me. Why would she bother unless she wanted to help James?

"You've made some progress. I had a feeling you might have. Good for you."

Was that a hint that she'd known all along? "I'd appreciate if you didn't share the news with anyone just yet."

She nodded. "You can trust me."

If only I had James's lie-detecting skills.

"Don't give up, Lily. We'll find James and punish those responsible. You have my word. In fact, I'll give you my witch's promise. Hold your palm up against mine." I did as she asked. "I, Angelica Constance DuPree, promise to do my utmost to catch and punish those responsible for kidnapping James Mathew Bianchi. I promise to be a trustworthy ally to you, Lily Katerina Bianchi in this matter. In the presence of Mother Earth and on my witch's power, so I declare."

Birdsong ceased. The light dimmed a shade, and the atmosphere thickened. Energy zapped through my palm, up my arm and stopped at my heart. "It's done." She drew her hand back and stood. "Enjoy your contemplation time. I'll be back to get you in thirty minutes, and we can go home."

"Okay, and thanks. I appreciate you doing that. Will you really lose all your powers if you go back on your word?"

"Yes. A witch doesn't make these promises lightly, but the need is great." She turned and made her way to the white monolith of a building, leaving me alone, just as I'd asked, well, except for Gus, who was hovering over near an oak tree.

Butterflies bumped around inside my stomach. I wasn't sure how I'd handle being in the place my brother had been taken from and beaten up, at the very least. If my hunch about my photos was wrong, we'd be back to square one, and if I was right…? What would I discover? *Please don't be evidence against Millicent.* If it had been her, wouldn't she do anything she could to stop me going there tomorrow? She knew my secret. *Crap.*

So, all I had to do was survive tonight. I could do that, right?

Yeah, I totally could.

CHAPTER 7

I hadn't bitten my nails since I was a child and my mum put that pepper-tasting stuff on them, but travelling in the back of the car with Millicent had me chewing for my life. Angelica sat in the front, and Jones drove. It sure was bright for six in the evening. Back at home, it would be way dark by now. I was having trouble adjusting to the seasonal difference. I yawned. And the time difference.

Thankfully, no one was in the mood for conversation. Before we left, I'd renewed my thought-containment spell so none of my thoughts would accidentally leak out to you know who. I glanced at Millicent out of the corner of my eye. I wanted to observe her without her noticing and starting a conversation I couldn't have.

She stared out the window, her hands playing with her phone in her lap, turning the device over and over and over. Snezana could have been lying about her and my brother having an argument, or maybe they'd had one—it just hadn't been as serious as she'd made out. If I backtracked one more step, I'd ask myself why Snezana wanted me to think their marriage was in trouble and that Millicent was so distraught she'd threatened him?

A: She could truly be trying to get me to find out more because Millicent was an evil husband murderer.

B: She wanted Millicent out of the way because she wanted her job.

C: She'd always hated Millicent. If so, why? Difference in personality? Jealous? But jealous of what? Millicent was pretty, but she wasn't as striking or modernly stylish as Snezana, and Snezana was a couple of years younger. Did their bosses prefer Millicent? Oh. My. God! My quick intake of breath was so loud in the quiet Mercedes that Angelica turned her head to look at me. I smiled. "Nothing to see here." She rolled her eyes and turned back around.

I couldn't believe I didn't realise earlier. Snezana coveted the one thing she absolutely couldn't have: James. That made so much sense. That woman had a crush on my brother. The things she'd said, which I'd thought so ridiculous, were so obvious. How had I missed it? Maybe jet lag had kicked my butt more than I thought.

I wanted to believe I had the answer, but I needed to be careful I didn't go down this thought path just because I wanted Millicent to be innocent. It seemed less likely I'd be murdered tonight, at least by Millicent. I hoped.

Jones dropped Angelica and me home first. "Good

night, Millicent. See you tomorrow morning." I gave her a smile and patted her arm. Her return smile was wan.

"Are you sure you don't want to have dinner with us?" Angelica asked.

"No, thanks. Today's been more emotionally taxing than I thought it would be. I'll see you both tomorrow, bright and early. Night." Jones shut the door and slid back into his seat. Angelica unlocked the house, and I stood and watched the car reverse down the driveway.

Angelica appeared at my side. "It was her first day back in the office since it happened."

"Oh. We shouldn't have let her go home by herself."

"She'll be okay. She's tougher than she looks."

"I sure hope so." I shivered—the night air had some bite.

I followed Angelica inside and locked the door behind us. Exhaustion had set in. It was 5:00 a.m. back home. Hello, jet lag. As soon as I'd eaten something, I was going to crash into bed. I crossed my fingers that tomorrow would be worth waking up for.

CHAPTER 8

The next morning, we were up at 4.30 a.m. Angelica was of the opinion we needed to do this super early to beat *those who would spy*. Whether she was talking about her boss or the bad guys, I had no idea. At least I'd gone to bed early, and it was 1.30 p.m. back home, so I was wide-awake. There was no way I'd survive getting out of bed that early otherwise.

Before we left, I recreated my mind-bubble. I also—shock, horror—had to drink instant coffee, as Angelica was a tea drinker, and there was no coffee machine to be had. Also, secret-expeditioners didn't do drive-through first, apparently.

Angelica came downstairs wearing black slacks, black long-sleeve T-shirt, and a heavy black jacket. I wore my black jeans, black jumper, and black ski-jacket. I giggled. By the time we got there, it would probably be daylight, and black was just as visible in the day. I guessed this was standard gear for anyone trying to sneak about the place.

We left via the back door. Angelica led us through a quaint cottage garden to the back fence and a gate that opened to a paddock. We turned left and followed the fence line for five minutes until it intersected with a country lane. There just happened to be a car waiting for us: a cute white mini. Angelica pulled keys from her pocket and clicked the fob. The lights flashed for a second, then she got into the driver's seat. I hopped into the front passenger seat, and we were off.

"Millicent's meeting us there. If anyone is watching her place, it will look too suspicious if we get her."

My gut feeling said to trust Millicent, but my logical brain said we should've been doing this without her, just in case. "Why are you so worried? At least you're supposed to be investigating." I didn't want to get in any trouble the Bureau, and this wasn't the best way to go about that.

"Ah, but we want to keep your secret, and if I'm questioned about anything, I can't lie to my boss. We take a witch-oath when we join. If I lied to him, I would lose my job immediately. I love my job."

"So you can't lie to anyone you work with?"

"I can, just not to my boss. Sometimes there are reasons I can't tell the truth to my underlings." Underlings? I chuckled quietly. I felt like I was in a spy movie spoof.

"I take it everyone has to take this oath?"

"Yes, but just to Drake Pembleton the Third. We'd lose

too many employees otherwise, and really, as long as he has the truth, the crimes will get solved."

Gee, that gave him a lot of power. Kind of scary, really.

It was just after 5.30 a.m. when Angelica turned right into a quiet residential street and pulled over. We got out of the car to delightful, dainty bird chirps. I smiled at the musical peep, peep noises, which were nothing like the thunderous prehistoric squawking of the raptors we called cockatoos or the maniacal kookaburra laughter that woke us most mornings.

The grey of dawn gave way to soft pinks and oranges, as the smattering of clouds came into relief against the deep-blue sky. Maybe I should start getting out and about earlier. I savoured the sting of crisp early morning air in my nose. Experiencing the glory of nature was a joyous way to begin the day.

I followed Angelica back the way we'd come. She crossed the road. Along the fence line of Deer Park was a small pedestrian gate. Angelica had explained Deer Park was a huge green space full of deer and nature walks. My brother lived not far from here, and this was his walk of choice every morning. We entered and followed a worn dirt path that led towards the interior of the park. It wasn't an immaculately groomed park: the grass wasn't as lush as at PIB headquarters, and clumps of wildflowers and weeds dotted the place.

Angelica walked to a large tree. "We're here, M."

Millicent stepped out from behind the trunk. She was

wearing blue jeans, black coat, black Wellington boots and a grim expression. "Thanks for doing this, Lily."

"What? You don't have to thank me! I'm doing this for me too, you know. If we don't get James back, I don't know what I'll do." I tried to stop my voice from wavering by making a fist with one hand and driving my nails into my palm. "He's all I have left."

Millicent walked over to me and shook her head. "You have me. Always." She hugged me, and I couldn't help the tears that escaped.

"Thank you. You'll always have me too." Unless she'd hurt him, then I'd have to retract, but at this point, I was pretty sure there was more to Snezana's comments than I could see. But I'd get to the bottom of it.

We continued into the park for another five minutes before we stopped. Angelica spread her arms wide. "It happened around here. We found traces of blood just there"—she pointed a few metres into the grass—"that we identified as James's." My heart kicked up a notch. I hesitantly walked to the patch of grass, not sure how I'd react to what I found, if, indeed, there was anything left to find. I looked closely. It might have even rained since his abduction, and I couldn't see anything that would indicate something violent and terrifying had happened here. I turned my camera on.

The moment of truth. I swallowed.

"Who's that?" Millicent squinted into the faint light towards the road, probably trying to see better. Four men in dark coats approached. One of them had his hand on his hip, just inside his coat, like it was resting on a gun. My heart rate kicked up a notch.

I looked at Angelica. "Should we run, or should you be casting a spell or something?"

Her mouth pressed into a thin line, and her brow wrinkled. "I know who it is, but I have no idea why they're here. Let me handle this." She turned to Millicent. "Don't say a word, dear. I have a bad feeling about this." Angelica walked towards the men, heading them off before they reached Millicent and me. They were far enough away that whatever they said only reached us in an incoherent low rumble. Angelica put her hands on her hips and stepped closer to the dark-haired man in front. I would not want to be him right now.

Millicent grabbed my arm. "Lily." She kept her voice low. "I know who they are. Two of them are PIB detectives. The other two are PIB police. I would say we're safe, because they're our guys, but I don't like the vibes coming off the whole thing."

"Why do you think they're here?"

"There are only two reasons they'd be here. Maybe they needed to check the scene of the crime again."

Hmm, that was only one reason. "What would be the other reason?"

Angelica turned and hurried towards us, the men marching behind her. It was like a wave of negativity rolling in. I had a feeling we were about to find out the second reason, and we weren't going to like it.

Angelica started speaking before she reached us.

"Ladies, I'm sorry, but this isn't good news. Just do what they say, and I'll get this straightened out as fast as I can." When she reached me, she reached out and grabbed my Nikon. "Give me this, Lily. You don't want it to get ruined. I'll make sure it's kept safe." Confused, I handed her my camera. And then I recognised two of the men. Adrenaline flooded my body. My mouth went dry. We were in serious trouble, and I had no idea why.

The hot guy with the dark hair from the other day stared into my eyes, his expression as hard as granite. That look made me want to run for my life. "Lily Katerina Bianchi, you're under arrest for hindering a PIB investigation and being an accessory after the fact in the disappearance of James Mathew Bianchi. Please turn around and put your hands behind your back. You do not have to say anything, but it may harm your defence if you do not mention when questioned something which you later rely on in court. Anything you do say may be given in evidence."

"Is that really necessary, William?" Angelica stayed next to me, glowering at the guy.

He blushed but didn't budge. Anger and fear churned inside me. How dare he accuse me of harming my own brother! I wasn't a criminal. "You couldn't be more wrong, mister. You're the dumbest policeman I've ever met if you think I'd hurt my brother or break the law in general. I'm a law-abiding citizen. I haven't even had a speeding fine. You're just a big bully. You think you're so tough with your handcuffs and gun, hiding behind your badge. Underneath it all, you're just some good-looking arsehole with a superiority complex. You don't scare me. I won't forget this. Ever. And when we find my brother, I'm going to tell him what a dick you were, and you'll have to apologise for arresting me. I might even sue the PIB for arresting me without evidence." Because, really what evidence could they have? I was innocent.

He tilted his head to the side, a snide smile oiling his face. "Oh, we have evidence. We're not some two-bit hack department. Now, would you like to do this the hard way, or are you going to comply?"

Angelica shook her head at me, and Blondie said, "I'm sorry, Lily. I don't like this any more than Angelica does. Just do as we ask, and it will go smoother." At least someone was being civil. I turned and did as asked.

William applied both cuffs in a second, managing to avoid touching me. That was skill right there. But it didn't impress me. "And don't even think of trying to use your magic. These cuffs block your access and give you a nasty electric shock if you try." Wow, dual-purpose handcuffs. The joy.

While I'd been ranting, Blondie had handcuffed Millicent. "Millicent Germaine Bianchi, you're under arrest for the kidnapping of James Mathew Bianchi." Her head was down as he read her Miranda rights. At the end, he whispered he was sorry. I knew which policeman I preferred.

Millicent went quietly. I'd go so far as to say she was dejected. Her shoulders were slumped, and each footstep almost dragged with apathy. How could she be giving up so easily? Unless she'd been expecting this? No, I refused to believe it. She was here, hoping to get more evidence. This was our one chance, and now it was gone.

At least it was early morning and there was no one around to see me get *helped* into the back of a dark sedan that was obviously an undercover cop car. William did my belt up for me.

"Gee thanks. Why bother? It's not like you care about my welfare." I squinted my eyes and willed him to feel all the hate I had.

He slammed the door and got into the front passenger seat.

As we drove to wherever the hell we were going, the fight seeped out of me. I'd missed my chance to really help James. Was he suffering in some dark basement somewhere, hungry and in pain, waiting for someone to come find him, each second dragging on like a year? Tears wanted to flood my eyes, but I refused. I wouldn't let them see me cry. They hadn't won. In fact, before I was done, they'd be on their hands and knees apologizing, and God help whoever sicked them onto Millicent and me. There wasn't a more stubborn star sign than Taurus.

Game on.

CHAPTER 9

When we got to the station, they confiscated my phone, saying it was evidence. They got me to put my palm on an iPad-looking black screen. It recorded data, which was supposedly my magicprint (like a fingerprint). Then they chucked me in a cell that smelled like a men's urinal. Ew. I scrunched my face in disgust. The guard explained all cells were warded against magic use before locking the door and leaving. Crap. What was going to happen when my mind shield dissipated? I was going to die. I knew not everyone could read minds, but any number of the guards or people coming and going might have that as their innate talent. Did that mean they weren't really using magic to do it? When I took photos, things just happened, and I wasn't even trying. If they pulled the wrong information out of my head, I was dead.

They'd kept Millicent and I separated, and I hadn't seen

her since the park. I hoped she was doing better than me. I felt like crap. This was humiliating, frustrating, and just plain wrong. At least I was in a cell by myself. Witch crimes must be thin on the ground right now.

After an hour or so, a young woman came and took me to an interrogation room. I couldn't get my head around this. How could I have been arrested? Even if I were released, would this go on a permanent record somewhere? Hmm, maybe not. This was the PIB, and wasn't it supposed to be a secret?

"I love what you've done with the place," I said as I sat. The cold interrogation room had more of the white-floor-white-walls theme going on, with a splash of vibrant colour in the grey plastic chairs and steel table. It had a morgue feeling to it. Lovely.

"That's good, because you're going to be here for a while." Ah, Mr. Crankypants himself. Thankfully, Angelica was with him. The girl who'd brought me here left and shut the door behind her. Angelica and Crankypants took seats opposite me at the table. I ignored him and gave Angelica a sad smile.

Her tone was kind when she spoke. "I have to ask you some questions. Please don't get upset." And this was off to a great start. "Do you know what happened to your brother?"

"No. The first I heard was when you showed up at my place." I tried to figure out how that could be a trick question, but it seemed okay. My leg bobbed up and down under the table.

"Do you think Millicent could have had something to do with his kidnapping?"

Oh, no. Not her too. What did Angelica know? "I don't think so. I don't know anything for sure, but Millicent loves James. They've never had any major problems that I could see, and she seems like a nice lady."

Crankypants leaned forward. "I sense a 'but' in there."

I made my voice as happy and innocent as possible. "Nope, no but." There was no way I could mention my conversation with Snezana. That was the last time I'd promise a witch anything.

"Ah, but I do think there's a but. In fact, I know there's a but."

My eyes widened. "You know about the conversation!"

He leaned back, his face slack with what I assumed was surprise. "You're admitting to your Skype conversation with Millicent?"

Oh, damn. My face fell. "No. What Skype conversation?"

"What conversation were you referring to, Lily?" He folded his arms.

"I can't say."

Angelica sat straighter. "What do you mean, you can't say?"

"On threat of death. I made a bargain with a witch—not Millicent, by the way. If I repeat any of the conversation or say who it was with, I'll die by choking. And to be honest, there are quicker, less painful ways to die. I'd like to experience one of those instead. But not right now. Just to be clear."

Angelica and William shared a concerned glance, and then William turned to me. "Do you always babble like a fishwife?"

"Are you always such a judgemental, insulting sour-puss?" I would've folded my arms too, but I had handcuffs on, so I glared instead. Don't think I hadn't considered kicking him under the table, but I didn't want to get arrested for that too, although it would have been good to get arrested for something I'd actually done.

Angelica stepped in, because this was clearly degener-ating into preschool territory. "Lily, do you recognise this conversation?" She slid my phone across the table. It was open on Skype, at a messaging conversation with Millicent. It was date stamped the day after James went missing.

MILLICENT: Hey, Lily. I've done something terrible. I hope you can forgive me.

LILY: Wot have you done?

MILLICENT: Don't do your nut, but I've hurt James. I might have killed him, but I'm not sure.

LILY: WOT!!!!!

MILLICENT: I can't tell you any more, but you have to believe I didn't meen to hurt him. He ran away, and now I can't find him. He's disapeered.

LILY: You gormless idiot! You'd better find him, and he better be alive. Don't talk to me again until he's found.

I blinked. I'd never had that conversation with Millicent. What the hell did "gormless" mean anyway? And who spells "what" and "mean" like that, not to mention "disapeered"? Something about the prose was familiar, but my memory was being its usual underperforming self. "I don't know how that got on my phone, but it never happened."

"So how did it get there?" I don't think William was looking for an answer. He'd already condemned me.

"I don't know. Is it possible for it to have been magicked there or maybe sent by someone with mad tech skills and access to one of Millicent's devices? And why do you have it in for me? What the hell did I ever do to you?"

His face reddened. "I don't have it in for you. I want to get to the bottom of this. James was... is one of my best friends. This is personal."

"I don't think it gets more personal than for me or Millicent, buddy. At least we were doing something constructive when you came along. If I didn't know better, I'd think someone was out to sabotage me. Maybe someone with a vendetta against Millicent." And there were my inner thoughts. They felt like the right answer. "Is *gormless* British slang?"

"Yes, albeit uncommon these days," Angelica said.

"Well, I'm an Aussie, and we don't use that expression. I've never heard it in my life. Hook me up to a lie detector if you don't believe me."

Agent Crankypant's smile was smug. "Take down your brain barrier, and let us ferret inside there, and I'll be satisfied."

"I can't do that. I'll die."

"Likely excuse."

Angelica turned to Agent Crankypants. "She's telling the truth. She couldn't have made all this up. She doesn't know our ways."

"Maybe she's playing you, Angelica. Maybe Millicent has educated her over the last few months. How would we know?"

Angelica kept her gaze on him. "So, you're saying Millicent premeditated this for months and was educating Lily in the meantime, just in case Millicent might want to confess later in a recorded conversation? A bit farfetched, don't you think?"

This was like a movie, when everything was on a speedy slide for the main character, and you knew they were going to through hell before they got to the happy ending. I always walked away and came back later. It wasn't something I handled well, and now I was living the nightmare. "You're my brother's best friend, supposedly. How did they seem as a couple to you?"

He looked at me, a begrudging expression of under-standing on his face. "They're lovey-dovey all the time. They'd do anything for each other. But people have secrets. Everyone does. What goes on behind closed doors isn't always what you think."

"I bet it is with them. James would've told me if they were having trouble. He's sounded happy every time I've spoken to him. Except..." And now I knew. I knew who'd done this. I should've realised earlier, because James had confided in me about his assistant, but he'd never named her, and it was only once, about two months ago. How could I have forgotten? Oh, yeah, crappy memory. And now it was my word against hers, and we had no clues. None. I had to remember what she'd said, word for word with that spell. I needed to see if there was any wiggle room, or there was no way I could tell them Snezana had used that phrase: don't do your nut. I shut my eyes and thought. We were in the cafeteria, and she'd held my hands.... That was it! Blah, blah, blah, *I will not repeat any part of this conversation to a living soul.* I groaned and opened my eyes. "I can't tell you all of it."

William shook his head. "About what I expected from you."

I opened my mouth in indignation. I'd be up for murder soon if he kept that up. "Well, you can stick your expecta- tions—" Angelica held up her hand for me to stop. Fine. I took a deep breath. "I can tell you what James told me about two months ago. He hadn't named her, but he was annoyed with his assistant. He'd said she kept flirting with him, and he'd taken to working out of the office to avoid her."

William shrugged. "He said the same to me a couple of times, but we laughed it off. It all seemed harmless. Are you suggesting Snezana is trying to frame Millicent to get her out of the way?" Bingo! The man's a genius.

She'd called her a bitch, but I couldn't say that either. Damn that choking spell.

Angelica shook her head. "I'm sorry to say, but that's not enough to convict anyone, and to be honest, it draws unwanted attention to the Bureau. We don't need a scandal like that."

"How is that a scandal? It's not like *he* harassed *her*."

Angelica's voice was kind, at least. "I'm sorry, Lily, but it's hearsay; James isn't here to verify it. There's no proof it even happened, let alone evidence she planted any evidence."

"Well, find some. That's what we might have done if we hadn't been arrested this morning. And who ordered the arrest? Don't tell me you found this Skype conversation at the last minute. You know what? I have no idea if she was spying on us, but I want my phone examined for a tracking or spying device, witchy or otherwise." I had no idea if they even existed, but stuff it. I was going there. I had nothing to lose. "How else were we conveniently located at just the right time this morning? Who sent you to get us?"

Angelica turned a stern eye on William. "I was wondering the same thing about the speed at which you turned up this morning. Who sent the order through to tail us?" She jerked her chin up and stared down her nose at him.

"Michael from dispatch called it through late last night, around 10:00 p.m. He said new evidence had come in, and we were to keep an eye on Lily. When you slipped out the back this morning, we were sitting down the road. Michael called through again and gave us the heads-up."

I slid my phone back across the table to Angelica. "Think you can check it out?"

"It would be my pleasure, Lily. I'm sorry, but you'll have to go back to your cell until we can sort this mess out."

Ever the joyful one, William said, "If we can sort it out."

My stomach fell. The person who wanted Millicent out of the way was in a position of power in this investigation, and who knew who else she had in her pocket. And through all this, where was James? Was he even alive? We were no closer to catching the kidnapper. Or were we? Why would Snezana set up Millicent but steer the investigation away from finding the man she coveted. Unless she knew where my brother was. *Oh, crap.*

"What happens if this doesn't get sorted out? Will I be in here forever?"

William stood and straightened his black tie. "Not forever, but if this goes to trial and you're convicted, you could get ten to twenty years."

My mouth dropped open. Ten to twenty years for nothing? My stomach roiled, and my head spun. I rested my head on my cuffed hands on the table. This couldn't happen. There had to be a way around it. I just had to think, and God knew I had plenty of time for that now.

Angelica patted my back. "Don't lose hope, Lily. We'll get your phone checked out and see what we come up with. When a witch uses their power on something, they leave behind a signature, like a fingerprint, but it fades after a few days."

I sat up. "I'm pretty sure that whoever did this would have set it up yesterday afternoon and made it look like the message was sent last week. Check Millicent's stuff for tampering as well."

"How can you know?" William stood behind his chair, his hands gripping the top of it.

Could I mention she'd asked about my phone or touched it? Yes, I could! She'd done that before she gagged me. I smiled, sparks of satisfaction bursting through me. "Because only one person's touched my phone, other than me, the whole time I've been here, and it just happened to be yesterday, around two or two thirty."

Angelica's eyes were bright. I wondered if she suspected.

"Snezana, James's assistant, the same one he must have been complaining about a couple of months ago." My smile was all satisfaction. Take that, you crazy witch.

Angelica smiled. "We have a long way to go to get this sorted, but thank you, Lily. I'll let you know as soon as we have some answers."

"Thanks. Oh, and since I can't redo my thought-cloaking spell, can you promise not to read my mind. I really, really don't want to die. Is there any way you can stop others from reading my mind?"

"I can ask, but there's no guarantees. I'll redo it for you now, and hopefully it will be good until tomorrow morning. We can figure something else out then, if you're still in here."

"Okay." That was better than nothing. She redid the protection, then they both left. The same woman from before came in to take me back to my cell.

I laid on the bed and shut my eyes: I didn't need to see

the two-metre-by-two-metre room with a toilet in the open and be reminded where I was. This place had video security. Great. They could see me going to the toilet. How long could I hold on until I wet myself? This was a nightmare. It didn't get any worse.

Was Snezana somewhere in this building watching Millicent and me in our cells and laughing? She was going to be so pissed when she found out I'd pointed the finger at her. I just hoped they'd find evidence of her tampering with my phone before she figured out how to make my life worse. She'd likely have some excuse for why she'd tampered with the electronics, but at least she'd get on Angelica's bad side. I imagined Angelica wouldn't take kindly to being spied on. And it would show stupid crapface policeman he was wrong about me. I'd enjoy rubbing his smug face in it.

It was frustrating to not know if my hunch was correct, but there must be something left to find out at the park, because assuming Snezana was trying to stop me from spending any time there—it seemed obvious to me at this point that's what she was doing—there must be evidence that could lead to her. Worst-case scenario, nothing would be found connecting the messages on my phone to Snezana, and my already dubious reputation would be unsalvageable. I might as well get used to peeing in public. And poor Tracy. She may have been the bride from hell, but she'd lost her father, and now I wasn't going to be able to get her photos to her anytime soon.

This was all because the stupid PIB had a shitty employee-screening process. How did a psychopathic bad speller make it in? Who spells "what" "wot"? Clearly someone who developed an inappropriate crush on their boss, kidnapped him, and then framed his wife and sister.

Maybe an hour had passed when I decided to stop worrying and waiting for news and have a nap. Things always looked better when you first woke up, unless you'd just had a nightmare. *Sigh. Let's not go there, Lily.* I needed a time out, and sleep was the only way I was going to get it.

So I thought about the last summer holiday I'd shared with James and my parents. We'd gone up the coast to Crescent Head—an awesome surf spot with cabins overlooking the waves. We'd spend all day surfing and swimming, and night-time brought barbeques with other families.

As I drifted off to sleep, I swore I could hear my mother's laughter and smell the salty spray. If I replayed these memories enough, they'd stay in my heart forever.

No matter how long I was imprisoned here, no one could ever take them away from me.

CHAPTER 10

I woke to a female guard putting a tray of dinner on the floor, another guard standing outside, just in case I attacked. This was ridiculous.

I sat up. There were no windows, so I had no idea what time it was. "Excuse me. What time is it?"

"5.15 p.m."

"And can you tell—" She stepped outside, clanged the door shut, and walked off. "…me when I might have some news," I finished quietly then sighed.

Dinner didn't smell like much. I knelt down and picked up the tray then placed it at the foot of my bed—if I spilled any dinner, I didn't want to have to sleep in it later. I removed the foil. Boiled broccoli, sporting a less than appetizing grey tinge, plain rice, fish fingers, and a cup of lukewarm tea, not coffee. For someone who wasn't in the mood to eat, this was not helping. My traitorous stomach grumbled nevertheless, as I hadn't eaten since last night.

I picked up the plastic fork and started eating—there was no telling when I'd get my next meal. After finishing dinner, I tried to ignore my bladder. It was screaming, "Please pee. Please pee. Please pee." I stared at the porcelain shrine to embarrassment against the wall. What if the guards came back when I was using it? Maybe they watched on a monitor in an office and waited till you went and came to watch on purpose. Those bastards! Okay, so this was all assumption right now, but I wouldn't put it past them.

I lay on my back, hoping it would quiet my screaming bladder. Some relief, but it wouldn't last long. I shouldn't have drunk the tea. I crossed one leg over the other and squeezed my pelvic floor. Then I shut my eyes and squeezed them too, because, you know, it might help.

Damn it!

I jumped up and grabbed my pillow. I held one of the short ends in my teeth, so the pillow covered my front, then pulled my jeans down. I sat quickly, holding the pillow as a shield the whole time. There was nothing to see here, folks. I managed to wipe myself and pull my jeans back up undercover. I washed my hands then sat back on my bed, proud of my resourcefulness.

Over the next couple of hours, I got off my bed and stretched as if I were going for a run, then I lay on the floor and did some push-ups, sit-ups, got up and did a few sets of lunges. I couldn't sit still for long, and I didn't want to lose my fitness. As I was jogging on the spot, a voice sounded from outside my cell. "Spending your time wisely, I see." Agent Crankypants. Had they found something?

I stopped jogging and turned around. Angelica was there too, standing just behind William, her face serious, but not unduly worried from what I could tell.

I grabbed my foot and pulled it behind myself to my bum for a quad stretch. I was going to play this as cool as possible. "I always spend my time wisely, but the question is, do you? Have you got some good news?"

His jaw muscles bulged as he clamped his teeth together. *He he.* Annoying him was way too easy but still lots of fun.

Angelica nudged him in his ribs with her elbow. He rubbed his side and looked at her. "Well, are you going to tell her or not, William?" She smiled sweetly at him.

He turned back to me. "It seems, Lily, that you were right."

Oof, that must have hurt to say. I tried not to smile too much. "You don't say."

He ignored my comment and continued. "Traces of magic were found on your phone and Millicent's desktop computer at home, but the magical fingerprint has been scrambled, so we can't say who did it. It's not enough to set you free, though, because we've found a magical tracking device on your phone, so the magical footprint could be from that. We can't prove the messages were magicked there too, at this stage."

"But what was magicked on Millicent's computer if it wasn't the messages?"

"We need longer to figure it out. It's with our second best tech guy, Peter."

"Why isn't it with the best tech guy you have?"

His cranky-pants mask slipped. The tension in his face slackened to sadness. "Because that's James. He's our best guy."

"Oh." Well, that answered that. "I have another question."

"Of course you do."

"Can you stop being such a crap head for two seconds? Actually, don't answer that—that wasn't my question, and I already know the answer."

He scowled, and Angelica smirked.

"If a message was magicked onto my phone, would it also go to my computer too, since that has Skype? I was thinking that if it was put there via magic, it wouldn't have gone through the normal system of message delivery, which means if I turned on my computer, the message wouldn't show up."

Angelica said, "But can't you delete Skype messages?"

"Yes, but then wouldn't I have deleted the one on my phone too? Supposedly, I've had all week to do it. Actually, I haven't had Skype turned on, on my iPad for about a month. You could turn it on where there's Wi-Fi and see what updates come through. That would prove it, wouldn't it?" Hope swelled my chest, fool that I was. It wasn't in my nature to give up.

Angelica nodded. "Well, then, I'm going home to get it. William can come with me as a witness, as we don't want any more accusations of tampering or favouritism." She rolled her eyes. I couldn't wait to find out what had happened for her to say that. "Where is the iPad, Lily?"

"In my knapsack on the bed. The passcode is 1920. Good luck. If you can prove the message wasn't real, can I get out of here tonight?"

"I don't want to promise anything, dear. Let's just go through one step at a time. I'm fighting with Snezana and Mr Pemberton on this. They're both beyond eager to catch someone."

"But what motive could I possibly have for protecting the person who hurt my brother? He's all I have left."

William was all too quick to jump in. "You could be mad at him for moving over here and leaving you. Maybe you think you'll get some kind of inheritance, or maybe you've become so close with Millicent that you wouldn't miss your brother."

"That's crazy talk! How could I stomach being friends with someone who hurt my brother? What the hell is wrong with you people?"

"You'd be surprised at what we see in this job, what motivates people. It's rather depressing. I wouldn't put anything past anyone, and I'm sorry if that upsets you, but naiveté gets you nowhere." He turned and walked away.

Wow, he was a sorry sack. I could understand that dealing with the evil-doers of the world every day would get you down, but of course there were still nice people who loved their families and their significant others and would never think to do anything horrible to them. If there weren't, what was the point of punishing the bad people? Why not just let everyone sort each other out and let the most evil one win, since no one deserved justice anyway? Life had really done a number on him.

"Lily." Angelica's voice came through my thoughts. "I'll come back as soon as I can. If we can get you out tonight, we will. I promise."

"Thanks." I smiled. "Good luck." I walked to the bars and whispered. "Don't trust the person the little birdie told you about. Please."

She nodded. "I'm way ahead of you. Now get some rest. I'll be back later."

I watched until she was out of sight and the outer door to the cells clanged shut. I felt like a puppy in a shelter. Gah, now I was going to feel sad about the puppies. If I didn't live in an apartment, I'd save two dogs as soon as I got home. Maybe I could just donate to the RSPCA, our animal protection society. I was so going to do that when I got out of here. But for now, it was back to squats.

A QUIET, METALLIC *TAP, TAP, TAP*, MADE ME OPEN MY EYES. The lights had been turned off, but the emergency exit signs in the hallway cast a faint glow.

"Hey, prisoner. How's it going?"

I sat up and squinted into the gloom. It didn't sound like Angelica. Bummer. Unfortunately, I finally recognised who that voice belonged to. "Hey, Snezana. What brings you down this way?" I was livid with her, but I wouldn't give her the satisfaction of seeing me riled up.

"Thought you'd want the latest information, future sister-in-law."

I shuddered. Whatever she had to say couldn't be good. She was clearly here to gloat. "I'm kind of busy right now. Could you come back later?"

She laughed. "Nice try, Lily. You don't fool me for a second. Are you telling me you don't want to know about the new evidence we found against Millicent?"

"I'm sure Ma'am will tell me when she gets back." My hackles rose. It took all my self-control to keep my voice even.

"Hmm, she might be a while. She's in getting a dressing down from our boss. He feels she's not an impartial party. She could compromise this whole investigation." Her teeth glowed white when she grinned. It was disconcerting.

"You really think you're going to get away with this?"

"Get away with what, my dear Lily? Exposing the truth? We'll find James soon, but if we don't, Millicent will still rot in jail forever. I'll be devastated if I never see him again, but at least I'll know I brought him justice."

"I know you tried to have me kidnapped and you sent those messages, and so does Angelica. Millicent and I will be out of here by tomorrow." Those words didn't sound as confident when I was locked in here and she was out there. And I may have assumed Angelica also thought Snezana was behind my kidnapping.

"Oh, darling, I didn't send anyone to kidnap you.

Having you here is way more fun. Didn't you hear me when I said there's new evidence? You need to pay better attention. You've missed your chance now. I'll be back tomorrow. Maybe you'll be in a better mood for visitors. Good night. Sweet dreams."

Again, the outer door clanged shut, leaving me in the dark, alone. How could that witch be getting away with all this when she couldn't even spell properly? *Could someone please wake up and figure this out?* If Angelica were running this place, the whole thing would be over by now. This was worse than an episode of *Days of Our Lives*.

There was a chance Snezana was exaggerating or making the whole thing up to scare me, but every minute Angelica didn't show up to get me out, the worse things looked.

I'd rested too much today to want to lie down again and was irritated from witch-face's visit, so I sat and leaned against the cold concrete wall. Why was she so hateful? It wasn't hard to be nice—millions of people did it every day. My goal in life, other than saving my brother, was to prove she was behind everything before she ruined three peoples' lives.

Light swept into the hallway. The door clanged shut. Who was it going to be this time? If it were Snezana, I'd do squats while she was watching, just to mess with her. I hopped off the bed as the footsteps tapped closer. They sounded more like flat shoes than heels.

A tall, broad-shouldered figure came into view. "Blondie?"

"Say what?" The blond policeman grinned.

"Oops. I was just excited to get a visitor I didn't hate. Sorry, I don't know your name."

"How remiss of me. I'm Beren. Pleased to formally meet you, Lily."

"Likewise. I'm almost scared to ask why you're here. Nothing seems to be going the right way today. Well, ever since Sunday, really."

"You have a knack for being in the middle of trouble."

"Hey, I didn't ask for any of this. It's the PIB's crappy employment procedures. I have nothing to with any of this, except as an innocent bystander."

"Shouldn't you be bystanding more and participating less?" He laughed.

"Believe me. I'm trying. So, have you come bearing good or bad tidings?"

"A bit of both, actually. How would you like to get out of here?"

"Is that a rhetorical question?"

He put a key in the lock and turned it. *Click.* He pushed the door open and swept his arm towards the hall. "Welcome back to the free world, Lily."

Sweet relief swept through me like a tsunami. Tears came unbidden as I stepped out of my cell.

"Are you okay?" Beren took one look at my face and enveloped me in a hug. Ooh, this was nice. Maybe my hug aversion didn't extend to attractive men with firm chests. I couldn't remember the last time I'd felt so safe. I snuggled in closer. Who was this wanton woman? Why was I suddenly hungry? Oh, that was wontons. One of these days I would stop being distracted by my stupid brain.

I sniffed. Would Beren be grossed out at having someone else's snot on his top? I leaned back. "I'll be okay. Thanks." He dropped his arms. No more warmth. Bummer. "So how come I'm getting out."

"Will sent me down here to get you. He's waiting outside in the car. Angelica's still in discussions with Mr Pembleton, trying to get Millicent out. They've agreed you can leave on the proviso that you stay inside Angelica's house until the case is solved. They don't trust you or your relationship with Millicent, hence the home detention until everything's sorted."

"So, they proved those messages were planted?"

"Yes."

"But they still think she could be guilty?"

"I can't comment any further, Lily. Sorry."

I followed him through the door. Argh, the bright lights, they burn. I squinted until my eyes adjusted to the change. "Can I see Millicent before we go? I want to make sure she's okay."

"I don't think that's a good idea. The boss is out for blood. The sooner you get out of here, the better. He may decide to put you back in the cell." Beren walked quickly to the lift. We went up a level—the cells were situated on a below-ground level, extra secure I supposed. We reached the ground floor, and he signed me out.

Once we were outside, I took a proper breath for the first time since this morning. The blessedly big sky stretched out in darkness above me, multiple universes worth of space. I wasn't claustrophobic, but contemplating life in a small cell could make anyone antsy. I grinned.

A black Range Rover pulled up next to us. Beren opened the rear passenger door. "Your chariot, my lady."

"Why thank you, sir knight." I stepped in as lady-like as I could, which wasn't easy since it was quite high off the ground. He shut the door behind me. The luxurious scent of leather and something primal and woodsy hit me. I breathed in, appreciating the lack of urinal tones.

Nice ride. Shame about the driver. William eyed me through the rear-view mirror. I put my belt on and folded my arms.

Beren jumped in next to William. "Hey, man. Ready to roll? Let's get this lovely lady out of here."

William grunted. He put the car into drive and headed for the main gates. If I never saw this place again, it wouldn't be too soon. As much as talking to him chafed like my thighs in summer, I needed to know the latest. "How'd Angelica manage to get me out?" I wasn't giving him any credit if I could help it.

"We went back to her place, got into your iPad, and when we started Skype, it updated everything that was on your phone... except that conversation. I'm sorry I was so hard on you earlier. You were telling the truth, and I didn't want to believe it." He looked annoyed, but whether it was with me or himself, I couldn't tell.

"Apology accepted." I was stubborn, but if someone made peace, I wasn't a grudge holder. "How come you didn't want to believe me? Do you think you have a sixth sense for compulsive liars or something?"

Beren laughed. "It's the fact that he has no idea. It's hard to trust most people in this line of business. But poor, old Willy has been burned off the job too, so he just doesn't trust anyone."

"Shut it, Beren."

"Aw, poor Willy's upset. Want Beren to kiss it better?" Beren made kissy noises. I laughed. William looked angry enough to punch him. And he did. *Whomp.* A jab to the ribs. Beren grunted.

Ouch. Maybe I did have my mother's psychic abilities. Or maybe it's what I would have done.

"Why is Millicent still locked up, and why is Angelica arguing with your boss if everything's been sorted?"

We exited the gates, William put his indicator on, and we turned right. "Because it hasn't all been sorted. Some lab reports came back today, and they've found a piece of jewellery after sifting through the dirt they dug up from the crime scene. It's Millicent's necklace. We're not sure how it got there, but Snezana hasn't touched that evidence, so we know she couldn't have planted it."

"Is the lab in-house?" I asked.

"Yes," William answered. "Why?"

"Maybe she has a friend down there. Have you asked Millicent any questions about her necklace yet? Like when was the last time she saw it."

Beren nodded. "Nice thinking, Lily. Maybe you should come work with us."

"Ew, no thanks." I realised how that sounded. "I mean, not because of working with you. That would probably be something I could endure." I smirked. Beren laughed, but William stuck with his on-the-verge-of-being-angry face. He probably kept that one on because he was likely to need to get his angry face on at any moment. "I don't like big organisations, especially not government ones. There's always some lazy bastard who takes credit for your work, not to mention Snezana."

"She's not so bad," said Beren.

"Yeah, if you like psychopaths. No thanks."

Beren made some cat yowling and hissing sounds and raked the air with his imaginary claws.

So original. "You'll see, Mr Hilarious. So, when are you guys going to watch the lab security videos?"

They shared a quick glance, and then William looked back at the road. "We're not. We'd need a warrant. We can't just spy on our guys whenever we want. And where's the evidence, Lily? All you have is a hunch, if I'm not mistaken. We all want to find your brother, but going around like a bull in a china shop is not going to help."

"Gah, that's the other reason I couldn't work for the PIB; your processes suck. I'd be eternally frustrated. So, once I'm at Angelica's, I won't be able to go anywhere, not even Costa?"

William's gaze met mine in the rear-view mirror. "No. You can't even go into Angelica's garden. We'll set an alarm ward which will alert us if you step foot outside the door."

God, those eyes were something else. Why did he have

to be such an annoying cranky pants? "What happens if I do it anyway?"

Beren laughed. "You do *not* want to do that, Lily. Our officers and agents have permission to shoot first and ask questions later—when you're dealing with witches, there's not telling what's going to happen. William and I aren't on duty twenty-four-seven. Anyone could be assigned to guard you. You can't risk it. Please don't."

I heavy sighed. "Okay." As far as I could see, the only person who could bring Snezana to justice was me, and I didn't mean that in an arrogant way. I was the only one who didn't have their hands tied, and I knew more than they did about the sort of person she was. I needed to get back to the park and take those photos. There was a way. I just had to find it.

Every now and then, I'd feel the heat of William's gaze on me. Stupid rear-view mirror. I couldn't meet his eyes— they did things to me, things I didn't want. Being attracted to someone who hated you was not a good look, plus I didn't like him as a person. How screwed up was that? Bloody idiot hormones. If I could just ignore him for long enough, this whole ordeal would be over, and I'd be back home, far, far away from him.

We finally pulled into Angelica's driveway. The lights were on in her house. Beren opened the car door for me. Such a gentleman. "Thanks." Angelica opened the front door and came out to meet us.

How did she get home so quickly? "Ma'am, what are

you doing home already? Weren't you in with the boss when we left?"

She shuddered. "Yes, no thanks for the reminder. That man has a bee in his bonnet. Snezana's his niece. He didn't appreciate me insinuating she hadn't vetted evidence properly."

Whoa! So that was how she got the job. Why was I surprised? I looked at William. His raised eyebrow and smirk smacked of an *I told you so*. I stuck my tongue out at him. The way he narrowed his eyes at me was more steamy than angry. Oh my. Time to go inside before I did something to embarrass myself. That escalated quickly, unless I was just misinterpreting his facial expressions, which was likely. What was wrong with me? This was neither the time nor the place. Maybe Snezana had put a spell on me, to keep me occupied with other things rather than putting her arse in jail. *You tell yourself that, Lily.*

"But how did you get home before us?"

"I *travelled*." Huh? "Witches can pop from one place to another. Come inside where it's warmer, and I'll explain it to you. Boys, thanks for bringing Lily home. You can set the wards once we're inside. And can you duck over to Millicent's and feed the dogs?"

"Will do, Ma'am," they answered simultaneously.

It was so good to be back. Funny how I'd only set foot inside this place for the first time yesterday and it was already beginning to feel like home. I ran to the fire in the living room and stuck my hands out to warm them. I could get used to this. Angelica came and stood beside me. "So, do you still want to know about travelling?"

"Yes please, if you don't mind explaining it."

"I would love to. I meant what I said the day I met you. I'm here to be your teacher, your mentor. I'm sorry I haven't kept you safe, but you've come to us at the worst possible time. James's kidnapping has all the hallmarks of a revenge attack. We thought we knew the gang who'd done it, but it seems as if the more we find, the less we know. As much as I don't want you in danger, you've been a big help. You've brought things to my attention I was conditioned to not see."

"You mean—"

"Yes. Now, about travelling. Witches have the ability to open a doorway or tunnel, if you will, to another place. Depending on how good one is at making the doorways, you'll move from one location in one step or many metres, hence the tunnel comparison. All witches have a room in their house called the *reception* room. Historians always think they're to receive guests the normal way, but witches created them. When I come home, I can only arrive in that room. Each witch will set up a spell containing the coordinates of that specific room, but there needs to be a receiving spell for anyone to pop in there. Most witches keep their reception room locked, sort of like a front door, since your friends, or enemies, could pop in at any time if they know the coordinates. That's why it's good not to give them out to people you don't know very well."

"Can witches travel to places other than people's houses?" This was interesting. Imagine all the travelling time I could save for work.

"Yes."

"And?"

She looked sheepish then she laughed. "I don't know why I still find this embarrassing. It's silly really. Public toilets. Not all public toilets, but we've spelled enough of them that we have a fairly wide network of drop-spots. You'll notice in the United Kingdom that there's usually a locked toilet that has an Out of Order sign. That's spelled to be there. We keep a cubicle free for emergencies of the travelling kind."

I snorted. "That's gross! Why toilets?"

"There's a lot of them." She shrugged. "I didn't make it up. Don't blame me." Still grinning, she shook her head. "Yes, it's gross."

"Is travelling easy?"

"No. And now isn't the time to teach you. You'll set the alarm off and have all of the PIB out looking for you. You need to stay here and wait this thing out. I promise I'm doing all I can to get things going in the right direction."

May as well try and learn all I could while I was cooped up here, at least until I managed to escape. "Can you teach me how to figure out if someone's spelled something?"

"Yes, I can. Figuring out who the magic belongs to is quite difficult, but recognising magic is one of the things all witches learn early on. Have you ever felt anything when a witch is casting a spell?"

"Yes, when you or *that other person* used magic on me, I

felt a tingle wherever the magic went—so, on my hands or head. Sometimes it's warmth as well."

"Very good. When a witch casts a spell, they're using their energy on it, and that leaves an imprint. The first thing to look for is how it makes your skin feel. That overt tingling or warmth won't be there—it will be subtler, and it fades with time. So if I do something like"—she picked up a small, white-and-black ceramic bird—"and do this." She mumbled, and the bird morphed into a living creature. It puffed its feathers out before shaking and settling. It preened itself, seemingly indifferent to us. "Touch it, and think about your connection to the power. Be one with nature, with the universe. Feel the energy surrounding the bird."

I slowly and gently placed my fingers on the bird's back and shut my eyes. Its smooth feathers radiated warmth. It really was alive. I pushed away the part of me that was having trouble believing it, because I needed to focus.

The fire crackled. I breathed in, the sharp tang of smoke filling my nose. I concentrated on my feet, on their connection to the floor, then on the fragile creature beneath my hand. Soft humming, two different tones, filled my senses, more vibration than sound. One was a delicate oscillation that filled my mind with the joy of flying, cool wind in my face, wings outstretched in a timeless act of defiance—what was gravity to a bird? The other fainter resonance was deeper, heavier, dark earth and boundless sky, fear and joy and everything in between. I grinned. I was actually doing this!

Now I had to find Angelica's magic. I imagined sinking

deeper into the stream of the bird's life essence. The image of a bright golden thread of light appeared in my mind. I opened my eyes. It was visible, overlaying the bird in a tangle. I leaned closer and followed the path the maze of light took. A pattern emerged. I had no idea what it meant, but at least I could see it.

Angelica smiled and said quietly, "Shut your eyes again and concentrate on making the image larger. We use this to focus on the pattern within the pattern. The pattern of light can tell us what the spell was, but it's on the thread itself, you'll find evidence of the witch who cast it—it's like a fingerprint. We have a database of magical fingerprints at PIB."

I shut my eyes and zoomed in, making one section of thread really big, like it was under a microscope. Symbol after symbol, lines, curves, intricate and simple covered the light's surface. Wow! Was it another language, a kind of hieroglyphic system? Whatever it was, it was stunning, prettier than a night sky flooded with stars.

I opened my eyes and grinned. I wanted to tell Angelica how incredible it all was, but, for the first time ever, I was lost for words in a good way.

She laughed. "I know. I remember my first time, and I still feel that way sometimes. Not every thread is golden, and some leave you wanting a shower rather than fill you with joy, but this is where we start. And did you notice two streams of energy?"

I nodded.

"One is the bird's, which you would know from what it

felt like, but the other is life itself, the river of energy which is always there and always will be. It's the heart and soul of our power. Now, let's put this sweet creature back to sleep." She simply said, "Finito," and the bird's velvety feathers changed to porcelain, although it was still warm.

I breathed deeply and let it out in a whoosh. "That was something else. Thank you."

"My pleasure. But you don't have to thank me, Lily. It's your heritage and the right of passage of every witch. To become your best self, you'll have to learn everything I can teach you about our power, and who knows, maybe you'll discover things to teach me."

"Um, yep. Don't hold your breath. I'm so far from that, it's not even funny."

"You'll get there. I'm sure of it. Now, let's think about getting to bed."

"It's definitely been a long day. What time is it?"

Angelica looked at her watch—yes, a watch. Not many people wore them anymore on account of phones and computers having the time, but Angelica was coolly old school. "2:00 a.m. Time for bed. I'll see you in the morning. And do not leave the house. I don't want to wake up and find you dead on the driveway."

I laughed, even though she probably wasn't joking. It was annoying being a stress-laugher. People thought I was making light of something when I was just coping. "I didn't realise you cared." If I was honest with myself, I didn't know what Angelica thought of me. One minute she was cold and cranky, the next, she was gentle and nurturing.

Her answer was a small smile. "Off to bed. If I'm not here when you wake up, there's breakfast stuff in the fridge. Good night."

"Night." I grabbed clean underwear and my pyjamas from my bag—I hadn't had time to unpack yet—and headed for the shower. My happiness at sleeping in a non-government-issue bed tonight was tempered by the knowledge that Millicent didn't get that luxury. James was God knew where, and his poor wife not only had to worry about him, but she was in jail for something she didn't do.

Snezana, you better watch out, because it's game on, witch.

CHAPTER 11

I shut my laptop. I hadn't woken till ten. Angelica had left a note saying she'd gone into work, so I was on my own for the day. After breakfast, I'd edited wedding photos for a few hours, but now my stomach was demanding food, and my brain wanted coffee. Bummer— there was only instant. I held back a scream. I wanted the real stuff, like with frothy milk and chocolate sprinkled on the top. Could I call for someone to grab me one? No, no I couldn't, because I didn't have anyone's number, and I hadn't sorted out the bloody roaming on my phone. I didn't even have the Wi-Fi password for Angelica's house. I could have sorted the roaming via my iPad, but that'd been confiscated as evidence. Gah.

Would the alarm go off if I just opened the front door? They wouldn't shoot me for standing inside the door, would they? Call me stupid, but there was only one way to find out. I undid the deadbolt and opened the door, staying behind it before sticking my head around, but still inside the doorframe, to look out the front. I couldn't hear an alarm, although, it may have been sounding at PIB headquarters. Okay, no one had appeared. I pulled up my big-girl pants and stood just inside the threshold. Hmm, not shot yet. That was a good sign.

"Hello!" I called out. "Anyone there? PIB peeps, are you there?" No one told me I couldn't say the initials. No normal person would know what I meant, so it should be fine. Still nothing. I needed proper coffee, dammit!

Stuff it. I sang, "You put your left foot in, you put your left foot out…" And then I did, right out the front door. The alarm sounded in an ear-exploding screech. I quickly pulled my foot in, and the caterwauling stopped. William and Beren appeared, guns pointed at my chest. My eyes widened. "What the ever-loving f—"

"Jesus, Lily! What are you doing?" Beren lowered his gun.

My heart was beating so hard that my pulse throbbed in my ears. They'd never really shoot me, would they? Best not to think too hard on that. "Thanks for coming." I smiled. "Can you guys do me a biggie and duck to Costa and grab me a large skim-milk cappuccino with extra chocolate on top?"

They looked at me like I'd lost my mind.

"What?"

Beren's mouth dropped open before he burst out laughing. William holstered his gun and put his hands on his hips, his eyes more grey thunderclouds than blue. "We could have killed you. Are you shitting me right now?"

"Angelica only has instant, and I neeeeed my coffee. I don't have anyone's number. I hate asking for favours, and I would've gone myself, but I'm bloody well locked up. And can I remind you that I haven't done anything wrong? This is a witch-hunt… like literally." I raised a brow, my left one. I was actually quite good at it.

William approached the house. "Get inside. We're not having this conversation out here." That didn't sound promising.

I made my way to the living room. William and Beren followed me in. Beren's blond, scruffy three-day growth, and his black uniform made him look rather hunky: his smile didn't hurt either. These two were like night and day: angry and happy: fun and grumpy: nice and mean. It was grumpy who spoke. "Don't ever do that again." He stalked over and loomed. Yep, it was definitely looming, and he'd obviously had lots of practice. No doubt it was an intimidation tactic, so I folded my arms, deflecting his negativity. "We're not your servants. We're supposed to be doing a job, and getting coffee isn't it. We could've killed you. Do you get that?"

Have you ever heard anyone say the vein in someone's neck was throbbing? Well, his was. *Throb, throb, throb.* Weird yet mesmerizing.

"Why would you shoot me? You two know me. You know I haven't done anything."

"It's our orders, Lily. If we don't follow orders, we could

lose our jobs, unless we had a damn good excuse. I don't want to shoot you, but—"

"Well, that's reassuring."

He rolled his eyes. "But, I will if I see you outside this house. Got it?"

"How am I supposed to contact you then, well, not you, because you're too cranky, but Beren or Angelica?"

Beren snorted. William magicked a phone out of thin air and handed it to me. It was an iPhone 5. "That's an old PIB issue we aren't using. All our numbers are programmed in. If you need anything, you can call. The passcode's 0000."

"That's not very secure. Aren't you guys supposed to be cutting edge?"

"I changed it before I gave it to you." Ooh, he was clever. Magicking a phone while simultaneously changing the passcode. That was actually cool.

"Thank you. I appreciate it." I turned to Beren, because William was hard work. "Thanks for not getting angry at me."

He grinned. "It's hard to be angry with you. You make me laugh."

"Aw, shucks. So, I was wondering…"

Beren laughed and shook his head. "Yes, Lily. I'll grab you a coffee from Costa."

"Thank you. Thank you. Thank you! You're the best." I threw my hands around his neck and gave him a huge hug then headed for the stairs. "I'll just grab you some money." He started to object, but I was already halfway up the stairs. Woohoo, I was getting coffee!

When I returned downstairs, Beren was gone. Sneaky man. I'd just give him the money when he returned. Someone else was still standing in the living room, though. William stared out the window, his arms folded, stretching his jacket over his well-formed shoulders. Did he ever just relax and enjoy the moment?

I sat in one of the chairs next to the fire. I didn't feel like arguing, and not engaging was the best way to do that. Whatever I said, he'd find a way to get angry about it. How had he been best friends with my brother? James was a kind, easygoing guy. Maybe that's why—yin and yang. James was probably the only one who could put up with him. *Oops.* I checked my thoughts were shielded. *Yep. Phew.* Although I didn't know if mind reading was one of his talents.

He finally left his post at the window and sat in the other seat next to the fire. "What were you doing at the park?" His gaze wasn't hostile anymore, thank God.

"Looking for clues. But we didn't get a chance to find anything before we were so rudely interrupted."

"What clues were you going to find after the PIB had combed over everything?"

"Why don't you ask Angelica?" I didn't know who to trust. I didn't want my secret talent out there until I knew how it worked. If Snezana found out, she'd find a way to make sure I never ever got to use it.

He watched the fire, the orange glow flickering over his features. "She wouldn't tell me."

Wow, she really had my back. Did that mean she didn't trust him either or was she just being careful? "I can't tell you either. Sorry."

"Fair enough." He stood and returned to the window.

A few awkward minutes later, Beren returned. "I have coffee!" He strode into the living room with three takeout cups. My hero! I grabbed mine and pretended to grab for a second one too. "Hey, they're not all for you."

"Just kidding." I grinned, carefully removed the lid and licked the hell out of it. Yum, that was soooo good.

Beren and William stared at me. Was this a slight against English sensibilities? "It's yummy. Have you ever tried it?"

"Only in private," said Beren.

"I don't care what anyone thinks. Let them stare." I licked once more for good measure and scrunched up my face at them. Even William managed a smile that time. Finally. "But seriously, sorry about this morning. Desperate times call for desperate measures. Thanks for saving my life and getting me a coffee. Quick question. How was it you were able to materialise outside and you didn't need the reception room?"

William answered. "We spelled an anchor point yesterday, before we left. They only last for a week or so."

"What's to stop people spelling an anchor point in someone's house when they're visiting?"

"Most witches have their houses spell protected against specific things—like unauthorised anchor-point spells. I'll be back in a sec." William headed towards the kitchen.

I sipped my coffee. "Mmm, this is good stuff. Thanks

again. How do you put up with him? You're so nice, and he's so cranky."

Beren's smile was fond. "He's a good guy underneath it all. He's in porcupine mode right now."

Huh? Oh, I got it. "Protecting himself by being prickly?"

"You got it."

William came back. "Time to go, B. Bye, Lily. If you need us for something *important*, just call."

"Thanks. Will do. See you both later." They locked the door behind them, and I returned to my spot by the fire. Now what? Sneaking out was going to be way, way harder than I thought. I could ask Angelica to help, but then I'd put her job in jeopardy. I couldn't get help from anyone, and I could also expect to be killed or horribly injured if I got caught. But there had to be a way. Mum always used to say nothing was impossible, and now I believed it too.

The first thing to figure out was what I could do with my magic. What talents did I have that I could use to escape and get to the park? I couldn't see how me seeing unusual things through my camera could help, but I must have other talents, surely?

Not knowing where to start, I soon grew frustrated. *Gah, enough of this.* I jumped up and went to the kitchen to throw my takeout cup away. I'd made it as far as the island bench when I saw it. My mouth made an O. Oh, boy, would you look at that. A big, beautiful, amazing coffee maker. Be still my beating heart. I ran over to it. Ooh, a note. I picked it off the top and read:

Thought this would help, because no matter what you say, coffee is not worth dying for.

William

I wouldn't go *that* far, but wow, Beren was right: the guy could be nice. That was actually quite sweet. And next to it was a packet of my favourite coffee grounds—Lavazza. When had he had the time to do this? *Oh, that's right, witchy skills.* I was so going to make myself a cup later. "Thank you, William, wherever you are." He probably couldn't hear me, but you never knew.

Invigorated, I ran upstairs to grab my camera. There was always the risk I'd get photos of something I didn't want to see: like Angelica making out with someone, ew, but I needed to practice so I knew what I was doing once I got back to the park.

Hmm, what if I focused on what or who I was looking for? That might help, and if it didn't, I'd figure something else out. I thought of Millicent, since she wasn't always here, and it wouldn't be as much of a coincidence if she turned up in a photo. I pocketed the lens cap and flicked the camera on. I turned the lens to a wider angle to take in as much of the room as I could. I clicked off a few shots—it was a pretty room after all—but nothing happened. Then I stopped clicking and just looked through the viewfinder.

"Show me Millicent," I whispered, picturing her face in my mind. I delved for the deep vibration of power that underpinned everything. I imagined scooping some into my fingers. "Show me Millicent, please." A tiny electrical shot zapped my fingers, and I clicked the shutter button. It was the back of Millicent from two mornings ago, sitting on one of the sofas watching my lesson with Angelica. I fist pumped the air. I did it! I freaking did it. I lowered the camera and did a little happy dance.

The fact that we'd all appeared was interesting. Gave a new meaning to *selfie*. I giggled.

So when I recalled a scene, it was the whole thing, not just one person. I put the camera back up to my face and tried again, but I moved to a different spot. Was it possible to replicate the same scene or was it a one-time-only deal? "Show me Millicent again, same as before." I dipped my imaginary hand into the power and started shooting. The same scene appeared. I snapped three photos and walked around. It was like looking at one of those 3D images. It was also spooky watching the three of us there, yet I was alone. I shivered.

Had James ever been here? "Show me James." Nothing happened. I moved around and pointed the camera at the entry. "Show me James." He appeared in the entry, Millicent in front of him, both facing the camera, grinning, probably saying hello to Angelica. It looked like it was in the last year or so, judging by Millicent's hair length. My brother looked so happy. I blinked back tears. I knew I missed him, but seeing him like this made me realise how much.

I lowered the camera, wiped my eyes with the back of my hand then looked at the picture on the camera screen. I zoomed into his handsome face. I knew he was my brother, but I wasn't biased, really. He'd always had girls hanging around, hoping he'd ask them out. He was a respectful person too, didn't trash talk girls. I used to hide and listen to him chatting with his friends. Okay, so I might have been perving on one specific friend, but whatever. What you saw was what you got with him. He didn't bitch about his mates, and he respected women. And that was probably why Snezana got the better of him. He wouldn't cheat on his wife, but he was too polite to tell Snezana to get lost. I vowed to be less polite in future.

At least I was learning how to control this particular talent, although it was still iffy. I couldn't see him in the living room, even though he'd likely been in there. I'd have to ask Angelica more about that later. She may even have some books I could read on magic. I wanted to learn everything.

I practiced some more and managed to get one photo of a party that was held here in the last few years and another photo of Millicent from the other day. Looked like there was some randomness about what appeared—it wasn't like a video where you could get a more complete idea of what was going on. But this would be enough to get clues to solve this case; I was sure of it.

Afterwards, I relaxed with a cosy mystery I'd had waiting on my Kindle app, and around dinnertime, when my stomach started complaining, I grabbed the phone William had given me and called Angelica. She picked up on the second ring. "Hey, Ma'am, it's me, Lily. Just wondering when you were coming home? And how's Millicent?"

"Hello, dear. Millicent's not doing so well. She's rather

depressed and not eating. Everything else is about as you'd expect. We haven't made much progress since last night." Her frustrated breath was loud enough to make it across the phone line. "I see you have the PIB spare."

"The PIB spare?"

"Yes, the phone."

"William was kind enough to get it for me. I may have annoyed him a bit this morning, but it's all fine now."

She laughed. "Beren told me what happened, and for your information, I'm laughing at how you push William's buttons, but you almost getting yourself shot is not funny. Don't do anything so foolish again. Do you understand me?" Her angry-matron tone was back.

"Yes, Ma'am. So, are you coming home soon? I'm kind of hungry, and it might be nice to eat dinner together and talk about *things*."

"I have a couple of bits and pieces to finish up here. I'll be home in forty minutes."

"Can you send my love to Millicent?"

"Yes, I can certainly do that. See you later, Lily."

"Bye."

I kept reading until she came home. She arrived in the reception room, and came out with Indian takeout. Yum! I loved Indian food. "Long commute?" I joked.

"The worst." We laughed. Witches had it good, except when someone was trying to frame or kidnap them.

We set the food up in the kitchen-cum-family room. It was another gorgeous space with white-painted exposed roof beams in a triangle pattern. The kitchen was modern with traditional touches, like marble benchtops, stone flag floors, and a double Belfast sink. The stainless steel cooker was huge with six gas hobs and a double oven underneath. To complete the luxurious yet rustic feel, a white timber island sat in the middle with four chairs against the breakfast bar part. I didn't cook much at home, but I wasn't averse to learning how. I just didn't have much opportunity to entertain. I could see some awesome get-togethers happening here. Maybe Angelica would let me have a welcome-home James party here after we found him. I swallowed the rush of sadness that moistened my eyes.

Once we were seated and both had food in our plates, I told her what I'd done with my day, other than annoy William. I took a deep breath then plunged right into sharing my secret. "So, my special talent. I'm ready to tell you."

She sat up straighter, if that were possible: she always looked alert, and I don't think I'd ever seen her slouch. "Go on. I'm listening."

"I can see things through my camera. It started the night before I met you. One of the people at the wedding looked see through, like a ghost, but when I looked at him without my camera, he was as solid as anything. The day we were at Sydney airport, his daughter rang to tell me he'd just died." I shut my eyes for a moment, tears burning behind my lids, then I took a deep breath and opened my eyes. "Then, when I came here, I saw a woman in the window of one of the shops I photographed, but she was dressed in turn-of-the-century clothes. When I put my camera down, she vanished. Then at PIB, in Millicent's office, I had an idea to find out if I could really see the past, and I saw Millicent and James in her office." Angelica nodded, her eyes bright. "It appears as if what I can see can be forced to some degree, too, but it doesn't work every time, and I can't choose what appears. Why is that?"

Angelica nodded then pursed her lips as she considered my question. "It could be one of two things. You weren't using specific spells to retrieve the information you wanted, and to be honest, you'd need a new spell for each new request, but if you had the time, you could do it. The other reason is that it can never be exact every time. What you're picking up on is the faded imprint of something that happened. When we go about our business, we leave an energy imprint, little bits of it all over the place. Sometimes we leave more energy than others—usually when we're particularly happy, angry, or scared, for instance. Times when we're using more emotional energy. That energy fades over time too, so something you may have easily picked up ten years ago, may only be able to be picked up one time out of twenty now, whereas, if you'd tried to pick it up soon after it happened, you'd end up seeing it five out ten times. And this is exciting, by the way. No witch has been able to see the past since your mother. You really give me hope, Lily. Your gift can help so many people." She clasped her hands under her chin and smiled.

Warm pride infused my cheeks, but the weight of responsibility and fear of not being able to use my magic properly sat like a stone in my stomach. "Thanks. And what you've said makes sense. There was also something from this afternoon. Hang on, and I'll show you what I got." I excused myself and went to the living room and grabbed my camera. I wasn't sure if I'd done a good job explaining things, so showing her seemed like the smart thing to do. I came back and handed her the camera. "Just scroll through from here. Press that button."

As she went through each picture, she nodded, until she reached the one with James and Millicent at the front door. Her mouth formed a large *O* and she put her palm against it. Tears glistened in her eyes. "I remember that day. They surprised me with a visit for my birthday. James is a truly special man, Lily. Your mother would be so proud of both of you if she were around to see you now."

"Were you close?"

Her smile said it all. "We were best friends. We spent a lot of time together when she worked at PIB, and even though she moved to Australia, we kept in touch, writing and then emailing when technology got to that point. She used to send me photos of you kids, all the milestones— birthdays, school awards, grand finals." Her voice softened. "I still miss her. When she and your father disappeared, I vowed to catch those responsible, but I'm ashamed to say, I've failed, but I haven't given up. I'll never give up, Lily. I promise you."

When she met my gaze, it was impossible to ignore the desperation and fire shining from them. This was one promise she would keep or die trying. "Thank you, Ma'am.

Mum would have been happy to know you were fighting for her. If there's anything I can do to help, let me know."

She sighed. "Your brother was helping me. That's why he agreed to take a job here. When he first went missing, I thought it might be related to that, but some clues pointed to a payback for criminals he convicted about eight months ago. But we followed all those leads, and they've gotten us nowhere."

"Is it safe to talk here?"

"Yes. My house is warded for eavesdropping."

"I'm sure we'd have all the evidence we'd need if I could just take some photos at the park."

"There's no way I can get you out of here. Snezana has been causing chaos down there. Her uncle is buying all her manure and then some. It's a mess."

"So, the only way to get me to the park is to discredit Snezana?"

"Pretty much."

As much as I hated going back to where I'd been imprisoned, it might be the only way. "Can you get me back into PIB?"

"Are you serious?"

"Yes. I haven't been banned from there, have I?"

"House arrest infers you can't go anywhere."

"Can you make a special request? The other option is getting those security tapes and watching footage of the lab. I wanted to go in and take some pictures, see if I could prove they'd planted Millicent's bracelet."

"Without any proof leading to a reasonable assumption, they won't let me see them."

"But you're the boss."

She smiled. "I have to follow the rules, Lily. Don't you see what happens when we don't?"

Yes, I saw. Snezana got to run riot. Okay, so she had a point. "I can't believe I'm about to suggest this, but why don't I 'escape' again, just enough that Beren and William have to arrest me and stick me back in the cell. Couldn't you get me into the lab then? Surely Snezana and Drake don't sleep at PIB. They must go home at some point. We'd make sure to tell Beren and William what we're doing, so they don't kill me by accident." I couldn't believe they'd do that on purpose, surely.

She nodded slowly. "That could work. Even if we can't use the evidence you find for PIB, it would give us something else to go on. If we could prove that someone had done something wrong, we would have enough to at least clear Millicent and get the person fired. Snezana would likely get away unscathed, but then we'd just need to get you freed. Then we could go get the important evidence from the park."

It was as if worms swarmed my stomach, masses of them, writhing and grossing me out. I was crazy to ask to go back to that tiny room. If I didn't get the photos we needed, I'd be stuck in there forever. I couldn't stuff this up.

"I'll contact William now. He can tell us if now's a good time. Lily, are you okay?"

I had no facial filter, and I was sure *I'm crapping myself* was written all over my face. "I could use some time to get used to the idea, but why waste time? We may as well get this over with. What have I got to lose, except ten years of my life?" *That's the spirit.* Would James do this for me? Yes, he would. That thought alone was enough to settle my nerves, well mostly.

Angelica got William on the phone, and within sixty seconds, he was knocking on the reception-room door. I waited in the living room while Angelica answered it. Beren and William marched into the room and straight over to me. William stood in front of me, arms folded—how unusual. "Are you crazy? You can't do this. If you fail, you'll go to jail for ten years or more. Have you thought about what that means, Lily? You're even more impulsive than your brother said. Honestly, this is a fool's errand."

"Of course I've thought this through." For all of five seconds. "And thanks for the vote of confidence. You don't think I can do this, do you?"

He scrubbed his hand through his thick locks. "Do what? Get some evidence somehow from inside PIB. Angelica didn't share the details, so I have no idea what you two have planned, and to be honest, I don't want to know. If Beren and I get questioned about this, for Angelica's sake, the less we know the better. Just don't do it. Whatever you're thinking, drop it."

"Who the hell are you to tell me what to do?"

His mouth dropped open. "I'm your brother's best friend. I'm supposed to protect you and Millicent, and I've fucked up royally with that. I can't let you put yourself in more danger, Lily. I just can't." His face softened, and for the first time, I saw the nice guy under the bluster. He did mean well, but it didn't matter. It wouldn't save my brother.

"You know he'd do the same for me. And what's the alternative? With Snezana running things as far as this investigation goes, and don't tell me she's only the coordinator, Millicent is going to go to jail, my brother will never be found, and I'm going to end up being ejected from the country, at the very least. Why do you think she's making sure I'm trapped here? She doesn't want me going to the park and getting something that's going to help us find my brother and maybe connect her to this whole thing."

"Something will come up."

"It won't."

"You're too impulsive, Lily. Learn patience, for goodness' sake."

"Now you sound like James. I'm sorry, but we don't have time. The longer it takes us to find James, the less likely it is he'll be alive. I'm not going to sit by and let something happen to him if I have a chance of helping him."

Beren put a hand on William's shoulder. "She makes some good points, Will. If you thought you could help, you would. And you will." He squeezed and dropped his hand. Beren looked at me. "I'll help, even if Will won't."

William huffed. "I'm in. But for the record, this is a stupidly dangerous thing you're doing, Lily. If this goes to hell, I'm definitely going to say I told you so."

I expelled a relieved breath. Not that I was desperate to throw myself back in jail, but it had to be done. I met

William's gaze and gave him a genuine smile. "Thank you. And just for the record, if I do stuff this up, you can tell me how crap I did as many times as you like. I won't even argue."

He returned the smile. "Why don't I believe that?"

I shrugged. "I have no idea."

Worry warred with need on Angelica's face. "So, we're decided?"

We all answered, "Yes," simultaneously.

"Don't forget my camera."

Angelica held it up, having just magicked it to her. "Done."

Beren gave me a hug. "Be careful, Lily."

"I will. Thanks."

"Let's go, B. We'll be outside, waiting for the alarm." William turned and led Beren outside.

Angelica turned to me. "Ready?"

I took a deep breath. "As I'll ever be."

I walked towards the front door, my heart hammering.

Well, here goes nothing.

CHAPTER 12

As soon as the alarm sounded, Beren and William cuffed me and zapped us all straight to jail. Thankfully, no one got shot, and by no one, I mean me. After being processed again, I ended up in the same cell as before. I'd have to add some homely touches soon and maybe do something about that wee smell. I'd spent almost as much time here as I had at Angelica's.

Sitting on the bed, I refused to contemplate being here indefinitely—there was no use worrying about something until it happened.

It took an hour, but Beren and William finally returned. They'd had to wait for Drake to go home. Snezana was already gone, thank God. William unlocked the door and entered the cell. What we were about to do was all for the security cameras. "Ma'am wants to question you. Turn around and put your hands behind your back."

I turned around and let him cuff me. This was getting to be a bad habit. The guys led me out and up to the top floor, to Angelica's office. She sat at her desk, glasses on, reading what looked like an internal report. She placed it on the table. "Please sit."

I sat and then she gave a nod. "You can stand up now. The security cameras have been 'fixed.' We've got fifteen minutes. We've had help from the inside, but the less you know, the better." I stood, and William removed my cuffs. Angelica handed me a blonde bob-style wig. I donned it, and then she handed me my camera. We were ready to roll.

We hurried back down to the first floor, down another long corridor to a grey door that said *Lab*. Angelica used her swipe card, and we entered. There was a series of four rooms along another corridor: Lab 1, Lab 2, Lab 3. I assumed the next door said Lab 4, but we didn't get that far. We went into Lab 3, and Angelica clapped twice. The lights went on. "This is where we do forensic soil testing. If we don't find anything here, we'll try the other labs, but this is our best bet."

I pocketed my lens cap, turned on my camera, and got to work. I didn't think of anything at first: maybe the universe would see fit to show me what I needed to know, but nothing happened. Of course not. I focused my thoughts on the river of power and Millicent's necklace. "Show me the necklace at the moment it came here." I almost jumped when a man popped up in front of me. He was about my height, wearing a white lab coat, and his mousy brown, shoulder-length hair was gathered in an elastic at the nape of his neck. He was standing next to a table that held a black garbage bag. He wore rubber gloves, and on his palm, as clean as anything, was what I assumed was Millicent's necklace, but I'd never seen it so I couldn't be sure. I clicked off a few photos with my wide angle, noticing the large white clock on the wall in the background showed the time and the date. Bingo!

I zoomed in on the necklace to make sure I got everything. I walked around him, still snapping. I took photos of the stainless steel bench, floor, bag. The other three quietly watched me. When I finished, I took the camera to Angelica and brought up the photos on the screen for her to scroll through. "Tell me if you need anything else."

As they looked at each photo, Angelica shook her head. "Brilliant work, Lily. Absolutely brilliant."

William pointed at one picture. "That's the bag with soil samples, yet the necklace is clean. It's in an evidence bag right now, still with dirt all over it. Damn!" He looked up at me. "So this is your super-secret-squirrel talent. Nice."

Ooh a compliment from crankypants himself—wonders would never cease—and he was kind of impressed, plus he said "squirrel." Day made.

I'd worried about the wrong people knowing my secret, but I was pretty sure at this point that I could trust Beren and William: Angelica did, and I trusted her now.

"Is there anything else you'd like me to try and get photos of?"

"Now that I know what your talent is, there's a million things I can think of. You're going to be sorry you let us in on your secret." William smiled.

Angelica kept my camera. "I'll get these photos loaded on my laptop, but we still can't take this evidence to Drake, and we'll need to get Lily out of jail. I hope they buy our excuse. And then there's the little matter of finding a way to get Lily to the scene of the crime."

Beren patted my shoulder. "Great work, Lily. At least we know where to start. That lab guy's name is Michael. It's time to do some digging, which is what I do best."

They ran me back down to the cells—we only had five minutes left, and the cameras would be back online. Once I was locked in, I went to bed. Nothing would happen tonight, maybe not even tomorrow. I figured Angelica had a plan to get me out of here at some point in the near future, but we hadn't had time to discuss anything before we came here. Yep, it was true: I was impulsive. There were worse things I could be, like a wanna-be husband-stealing psycho-pathic kidnapper.

Before drifting off, I ran through what I'd seen in the lab. Why would Michael agree to help Snezana? Did she have something over on him? Were they best friends or in a relationship? Which would be totally fake on her part because she was in love with my brother, but she was the manipulation queen, so it was a definite avenue, or maybe he was just a sucker with a crush. You couldn't help bad taste.

I yawned. Today had been exhausting. Time to turn my brain off and get a few hours' sleep. "Goodnight, James," I whispered. "We're coming, buddy. Hang on."

CHAPTER 13

I endured breakfast without coffee. The porridge was fine, but tea wasn't my thing. I drank it anyway, because it had some caffeine in it, and I wasn't in the mood for a migraine. Using the toilet the second time around was just as disconcerting—like being in a dream where there's no toilet door. Thank God for my pillow.

Bored and sick of wondering when someone would show up, I launched into my exercise routine, starting with stretches. I managed the whole thing today. That was a bad sign.

Lunch arrived—a cheese and salad sandwich. That wasn't bad. It was just like a day at work, as I often made myself one for lunch. If I shut my eyes and blocked my nose, I could pretend I was sitting at my dining room table in Sydney.

I'd barely finished my sandwich when a pair of guards I

didn't know came to my cell. One was a dark-skinned lady in her twenties, about my height, who looked fit enough to take on her companion, a thirty-something white guy with muscles almost as big as Beren's. She unlocked the door. "Miss Bianchi, I'm agent Sophia Clarke. We're here to take you to Mr Pembleton the Third. Please turn around so I can cuff you." At least she was polite and didn't seem to hate me. I complied.

They walked on either side of me through the pristine white hallways. Looked like we were back at the meeting room from yesterday, or was that the day before? I was losing track of days, which wasn't surprising since I'd spent a lot of my time in a windowless cell. This was certainly nothing like I expected when I first heard I was coming to England. I never envisaged that helping find my brother would involve incarceration, among other things.

Sophia knocked and then opened the door. It was like a replay from last time. The old gang was here, even Timothy, who gave me a small, reassuring smile. Snezana sat next to her uncle this time, and there were no smiles or invitations to sit next to her. In fact, she wore a lovely scowl. With a bit of luck, she'd not only gotten up on the wrong side of the bed, but she'd also stepped in cat vomit doing it. Angelica gave nothing away: her poker face was back.

Sophia stood me in front of Drake, next to a seat that was already pulled out. Drake ran his hand down his red tie. His expression was sombre. "Please, take a seat, Miss Bianchi."

I sat but had to lean forward because of the stupid cuffs. How undignified.

"To be honest, when I gave permission for you to leave, I didn't expect to see you back so soon. James always spoke so highly of you, but you're not quite the well-behaved girl he spoke of. Nevertheless, Angelica has assured me the latest infringement was an accident." He glanced at her before looking back to me. "She even assented to a lie-detector spell." How had she pulled that off? I'd have to ask her later. "We've also had new information come to light proving that you haven't been involved in any way on any cover-up." This time, his glance was directed at his niece. She ignored him and inspected her red fingernails. He gestured to Sophia, and she undid the cuffs. "I'm very sorry for your treatment, Lily. Please accept my sincerest apology on behalf of the Bureau."

I rubbed my wrists. Could I accept his apology? This had to be the absolute worst experience of my life, and what about Millicent? I decided to take the high road, because we still needed to get my sister-in-law out. "I have to say, Mr Pembleton, I'm disappointed in my treatment, but I understand we all make mistakes, and I accept your apology. Thank you." He nodded. "Am I free to go?"

"Certainly, Miss Bianchi. William has the car outside, waiting." He slid a piece of paper and pen across the table and handed me an envelope. "Please sign this waiver, absolving the PIB of any wrongdoing and agreeing to not mention anything you've seen or experienced whilst you've been here, and you can have what's in the envelope."

My eyes widened. They were paying me off? I opened the envelope to a thick wad of gorgeous red fifty-pound notes. But they'd still done the wrong thing. What if they did it to someone who didn't have friends on the inside who could help? I looked to Angelica for guidance. She gave a half nod, which I was pretty sure meant take the money and run.

"There's ten-thousand pounds in there, Lily. I think that's fair compensation for two days of your life and any residual nightmares that will surely fade in time."

You know what? I was going to take that money, but I was still going to come back and witch-slap his niece. She was going down, and when I got my brother and Millicent out, we would all enjoy the ten thousand, which was actually about seventeen thousand Australian dollars. Our dollar was so crap. It was nice to think my suffering was worth more over here.

I quickly read the two-page document and signed down the bottom. "Done."

Drake and I both stood, and he held out his hand. "Safe travels, Lily. And rest assured, we're doing all we can to find your brother."

I shook his hand. "Thank you, sir. I have a feeling he'll be found very soon." I smiled and turned to Snezana. "It'll be so good to see him back with his wife, won't it? I just know how much he adores Millicent. I bet she's what's keeping him going, wherever he is." Snezana's face turned red from the neck up. She so wanted to kill me right now. *Go on, witch, try it, while everyone's watching.*

"Time to go, Lily," Angelica called from the other side of the table.

Sophia held the door open. That must be my cue. The two guards took me downstairs, signed me out, and stayed with me until we reached William's PIB-issue black Range Rover. Beren jumped out. "Thanks, Sophie. Adam. We'll take it from here."

"Right you are, Beren," said Sophie before they turned and went back inside.

Beren's grin as he opened my door was infectious. I grinned back and got in. I was free. *Woohoo!* In a moment of déjà vu, I strapped myself in and met William's solemn eyes in the rear-view mirror. "Please stay out of here this time."

"I'm planning on it."

William started the engine and accelerated towards the gates.

"Here's your camera. Angelica asked us to give it to you." Beren turned and handed it to me. *My baby!* I clutched it to my chest. "Those photos from the lab got you out of here. Angelica had to show them to Drake. They've arrested Michael, but he won't talk, says he's spelled to die if he breathes a word of anything. Looks like he'll take the rap all by himself. Drake wants it all kept hush-hush. If the higher-ups find out the lab was compromised, he'll lose his job."

"Well, that sounds familiar." Snezana was something else. "Does Drake know his niece is pure evil?"

William shot me a glance in the mirror. "He didn't get where he is by being stupid, but I'm sure he's doing his best to look the other way for as long as he can. Plus, there's no obvious evidence she's actually involved in any of this."

"What about Millicent?"

"They're doing final checks, but she should be out tonight," said Beren.

The burn of tears stung my eyes. Thank God. Some of the tension in my shoulders melted away. One down, one to go. "Thanks for helping. I know you both risked your jobs to do this."

"It's nothing, Lily. We'd do it all again in a heartbeat." Beren turned and gave me a smile, then firmly elbowed William.

"Ow. Yeah, yeah, we would. Milly and James are like family to both of us. This whole thing's been a nightmare."

Hmm. "Do you guys have much on this afternoon?"

William eyed me in the mirror. "I hate to ask, but why?"

"I would love to grab a takeaway coffee from Costa, and then I thought we could visit the scene of the crime." No one said anything. "Don't chicken out on me now, guys. I haven't been banned from going anywhere. You know this could give you the breakthrough we need. Think of James."

William groaned but turned right instead of left at the next intersection.

"Yes!" I couldn't resist a fist pump.

Soon the car was filled with the delicious smell of coffee, although Beren got tea. "Letting the team down, B," I said.

"Tea's in my blood."

"Don't worry, Lily. More coffee for us." William held his cup up in a cheers gesture. I smiled, happiness coursing through my system with the caffeine. This could be it. The day we get a strong lead on where my brother was, and maybe by the time I got home, Millicent would be there—surely she didn't want to be by herself as soon as she got out of Hotel PIB?

I drained the last of my coffee as we pulled up across the street from the park. Clouds muted the sunlight, casting a sombre glow across the landscape. I jumped out and placed my camera strap around my neck and turned the camera on. Lens cap in pocket, I crossed the road, William and Beren behind me. I was taking the lead on this. I couldn't wait: we were so close. I looked into the sky. Good. There weren't any rogue lightning bolts, dragons, or meteors heading our way. Honestly, at this point, I wouldn't be surprised.

I scoped things out through my viewfinder before reaching the gate. "Show me James the moment he was kidnapped." Nothing happened. My heart raced, and my mouth went dry. I was torn, needing to see and not wanting to. Maybe that was affecting things. I took a deep breath, thought of finding him and blocked out the part of me that would hate what I might see. "Show me James being attacked."

The light changed to a filtered early morning yellowish orange. Racing towards us, frozen with haunches bunched about to jump the fence were James's dogs. Further into the park, framed behind a cloudless sky were three men standing together and someone standing just to the side of them. I was too far away to see what they were doing.

I sightlessly fumbled with the gate, never taking my gaze from the group or my finger off the shutter button. I snapped a couple of pics in case they disappeared. The gate latch finally undid with a tink. I pushed the gate open and jogged towards the scene, clicking as I ran. This was the longest four-hundred metres I'd ever run.

Oh, God. James was hunched over, gripping his thigh, his face contorted in pain. Two huge thugs stood next to him, one on either side. One held the dagger hilt that stuck out of my brother's thigh, the other gripped James's bicep. There was the snake tattoo on the hand of the guy stabbing James. A jolt of pain scored across my heart, and I bit back angry tears. Bastards.

Standing, watching the whole thing with fervour in her eyes and a satisfied smirk on her lips was Snezana. *Click. Click. Click.*

I walked the perimeter of the attack, shooting from every angle. I recorded every face, every expanse of exposed skin, the denim jeans and black coats of the attackers, the blood staining my brother's grey tracksuit pants, the joy and mania on Snezana's face.

My breath came in pants. I reached Snezana again and looked into her crazy eyes. I wanted to break her nose, smash her face into the mud and grind it in, stab her in the thigh, like her thugs were doing to my brother.

But she wasn't really there.

I lowered the camera and tried to get my breathing under control. Unfortunately, there was no controlling the stupid tear that tracked down my cheek. "She's going down."

William and Beren stood staring at me. Of course, they had no idea what I'd seen—all they saw was me worked into a frenzy.

"What did you see?" William stepped towards me, his brows furrowed.

A violent shiver stung the back of my neck and raced down my spine. I drew in a quick breath.

Someone was using magic.

Snezana appeared next to me, her gaze just as insane as when she'd been here with my brother. My mouth dropped open—this wasn't an image of the past, but the flesh-and-blood real-time version. I jumped back. She seized my arm. Instinct kicked in, and I grabbed the camera from around my neck and threw it at William. He caught it just as darkness swept away the light.

CHAPTER 14

We must have been in a *doorway.* In four steps, she'd dragged me into a dimly lit bunker-looking room, with grey concrete walls and ceiling, and a dusty concrete floor. The stench of damp hit me. I stumbled, then Snezana shoved me to the ground. I landed on my hands and knees. Snezana kicked the back of my thigh. Fiery pain scorched up my leg to my lower back. *Son of a witch!*

Before I had a chance to react, she yanked my arms back and slapped handcuffs on me. "Ow." I fell to the floor, face first. Thank God my chest took the brunt of the fall—it still hurt, but not as much as breaking my face on the concrete. It was the first time I was glad for my C cups; normally they got in the way when I was exercising.

My shoulders ached from being pulled back too hard. And now I had no chance to magic myself out of this. Even if I didn't know how to magic properly, I could have tried something.

I rolled over and sat up. A dirty double-size mattress lay in the corner, a body sprawled on it. Oh my God. James. He was as still as a pond on a windless day—his eyes closed, his hands cuffed and resting on his stomach. Shit. Was he even alive? I watched for the rise and fall of his chest. *Please, please, please.*

Snezana grabbed my ponytail and yanked my head back, forcing me to meet her bulging, crazy eyes. "You couldn't leave it alone, could you? The problem is, I don't want to keep you. I only want to keep him." She looked at my brother, a dreamy look coming over her face. When she turned to me again, her face turned agro. Freaky scary mood change. "But how am I going to get rid of your meddling Aussie arse?"

If there's anything I'd learnt from watching crime shows, it was to keep the perp talking to stall for time. Because that's all I had right now. "Maybe you should keep me around. I can cook, tidy up." I tried not to laugh. They were my two crappest things, but she didn't deserve my best, and I'd enjoy spitting in her food when she wasn't looking.

"Three's a crowd, honey."

"But I know how James likes his food cooked."

She stared at me, probably sizing up if the new information was any benefit to her.

"Plus, James would be pissed if he found out you killed me. He'd never talk to you again."

That really got her attention. She narrowed her eyes

then spun around. She stopped at the foot of the mattress, knelt on it, bent and licked James's face from his jaw to his eye. *Ew.* I pulled a face. I couldn't help it. He was so going to want to bleach his skin when I told him. Snezana planted an open-mouthed kiss on his lips—*double ew*—before she stood and headed for the other side of the room where there was a door I hadn't noticed before. Without a word, she left.

I stood and went to James. Knees-first, I dropped onto the edge of the mattress and pressed my ear on his chest, above his heart. Relief washed through me. He was breathing. Thank God. His face was pale, with the exception of a bruised right cheek, his dark hair knotted. She obviously hadn't shaved him since bringing him here—his face was dirty, and his stubble was on its way to being a beard.

His leg was bandaged, but I had no idea if she'd cleaned or stitched the wound. What if it were infected? I went to put my cheek against his but remembered Snezana had just licked it. I shuddered and placed my cheek against his other cheek, which was quite tricky since I had no hands to hold myself up with. I ended up falling onto his chest. "Sorry, buddy. James, it's me, Lily. Just checking your temperature. I'm using a trendy new way they invented for people without arms." He didn't stir, but he didn't seem to have a fever, so that was good.

I stayed on top of him for a minute, just revelling in being with my brother. It had been too long since I'd seen him. Tears, yet again, worked their way out of my eyes. "I wasn't sure I'd ever see you again, but I made it. You can thank me later." I sniffled then wiggled backwards until I managed to sit again. "What has she done to you?"

How was she keeping him asleep? It could be a spell or drugs, or maybe those guys had bashed him unconscious. I couldn't see any blood in his hair, but that didn't mean he didn't have a big egg in there somewhere. Damn. I had no hands to check with.

I took a deep breath and looked around. Was there any way out of here other than the door Snezana had used? There was a long, narrow, filthy window just under the ceiling on the other side of the room through which I could see vague outlines of what was probably the ground. This room had to be underground. And that was it. The only way out was through the door and the snake's lair.

It was getting to evening, so she wouldn't be going back to work. I had to be prepared for her to come back. What if she planned on killing me tonight? Yikes. I had to get us out of here. I wondered if William and Beren had any way of following her. If not, I was so screwed.

At least they had my camera. There wasn't any evidence of where she'd taken me, but there was enough evidence to put Snezana in jail for a long time. Hopefully they'd be able to track the thugs down and figure out where we were from that. Unless the guys waited at the office and threatened it out of her tomorrow morning.

But by then, it might be too late.

Crap.

Double crap. I needed to go to the toilet. Messing up witch-face's floor didn't bother me, but how was I supposed to get my jeans pulled down with my hands behind my back? There was no way I could undo the button. I so needed James to wake up. "James. James, wake up." Nothing. "James, this is your annoying little sister begging you to wake up." His eyes stayed closed, his thick dark lashes I had always been jealous of resting against the top of his cheeks. I shook my head, sadness settling over me like a heavy blanket. I had to do better.

I shut my eyes and looked for the river of power, listened for the deep hum. I could sense it beyond an invisible barrier, which would be the handcuffs. No shock, thank goodness. Maybe you only got the pain if you tried to do magic rather than search for the power.

There could be a gap somewhere. Surely these weren't perfect. I shut my eyes and investigated further. Nope. There was nothing I could sense that constituted a fault I could take advantage of. Bummer. Maybe I should try the old-fashioned thing and attempt to get the cuffs off.

I stood and searched around for anything that might help. I walked the perimeter of the room and tried not to cry. Nothing but walls, floor, and my brother. I backed up to the wall. Pushing the chains linking the two bracelets together with my thumb against the wall, I rubbed it up and down. If I could keep it up long enough, maybe I'd wear it out.

After a few minutes, I tried to look over my shoulder to see if I'd made any headway, but the damn cuffs stayed out of sight. Times like this, it would have been useful to be a contortionist. Actually, a contortionist would have gotten their hands to the front and would have been able to undo their jeans button. Instead of looking at the cuffs, I ran my thumbs over the chain. Instead of being smooth, there were tiny ridges, but nothing more than scratches. It might take me years to escape this way.

I swallowed my scream of frustration. *Think, Lily.*

The door opened. *Crap.*

Witch-face walked in with a needle and syringe. A really big one. Was that for me or James? I did my best not to show fear—psychopaths lapped that crap up. I would not give her the pleasure. She wiggled her fingers at me. Pain slammed into my stomach as if I'd been punched. I cried out, double over, and fell to my knees. "Argh!" Knees hitting concrete was freaking painful too. I tried to breathe, but it wasn't easy. I forced myself to raise my head so I could see what she was doing to my brother.

She had the needle poised at the inside of his elbow.

"What are you doing?" I didn't expect her to answer, but I had to ask.

"He needs to sleep just a while longer. Soon we'll be able to be together as man and wife, but I have some things to take care of first." Her chuckle froze my blood. "You'll be happy to know, I've decided what I want to do with you."

I swallowed.

"James never needs to know I've killed you. But I'll have to do it now while he's asleep."

My legs turned to jelly. If I hadn't already been kneeling, I would've keeled over. Jesus. I couldn't let this happen. This witch was not going to kill me. Stuff her and her lunatic desires. "You know, if you make a mess, you'll never get the stains out of the concrete, and James isn't stupid. He'll know something happened here."

"I really don't care. I know you're stalling for time, Lily. You're a dead woman kneeling." She laughed. "See, I have a sense of humour. I'm a lot of fun, and you could've been my friend, but you ruined it. Stupid girl." She stood and walked over to me. I struggled to get up. I would not die kneeling before her.

I managed to right myself just as she reached me. She gripped my neck with her long skinny fingers. "Hmm, how will I do this? I do have a thing for choking, as you've probably realised. I'm not one for messes, and blood might get on my jeans, and these are my favourite pair."

Anger boiled inside me. Before I could stop myself, I spat in her face. "Ugly cow. Screw you!" Her face reddened like it had in the conference room earlier today. "Yeah, you heard me. Ugly, vile, disgusting. Not only does that describe you, but you're going down. You'll never spend any time with my brother. None. He'd rather be dead than with you, so I've decided to tell you my big secret."

She had her hands on her ears. "I'm not listening. La, la, la, la, la, la, la, la."

It was my turn to laugh. If this was the only way to hurt her, I was going to inflict as much pain as I could before I died. "You know what my special talent is?" She la-la-d louder. I could yell. *Just watch me.* "I can see the past with my camera. I have photos of you and your two goons kidnapping my brother. William and Beren have that camera, and I bet they've already shown it to your uncle."

Her la las mustn't have been loud enough, because her face paled, and her hands dropped to her sides. "You're lying."

"Ha! You wish. You stood there while the guy with the snake tattoo stabbed him in the thigh. You with your stupid crazy face."

"How dare you?" she shrieked, then slapped my cheek. The sting radiated over the side of my face, and I gritted my teeth. "You can't have that talent. No one's been able to see the past or read the future since…."

I smirked and pushed down the sorrow that threatened to swallow me every time I thought of my parents. "My mother."

She grabbed my throat with both hands, squeezing. I kneed her in the vagina—yep, no balls but it still hurt worse than waxing. Her hold loosened, and I barged forward, trying to chest her out of the way. Once I was past, I ran for the door she'd left open. I probably wouldn't get far, but try telling my survival instincts that.

I was almost at the door! Just a few more steps. *Crackle. Crackle.* I could feel my hair lifting as static charged the air. My body froze, and I flew forward, the momentum of my flight actually making me fly. Great. This was going to hurt like a—" I smashed into the ground, my chest and face taking the impact. Sharp pain shot through my boobs and jaw. I hoped nothing was broken.

Snezana's pink stilettos appeared in front of my face.

She used one of her shiny shoes to push me onto my back. She started laughing. Her laughter grew until she was doubled over with tears pouring down her face. She slowly straightened and daintily dabbed at her face, obviously avoiding smooshing her make-up. Seriously? What did it matter what she looked like? Her only company was an unconscious person and someone who was about to be dead.

"Oh, you look hilarious lying on the floor in that running position with your legs bent. Not going very far, are you?"

I felt ridiculous, but I wasn't going to admit it. "It's quite comfortable actually. Who knew?"

She clenched her fists. "Enough! Time to die." Her fingers wiggled. The air pressure built, and the static was back. My skin warmed. Then it got hotter, like I was standing too close to a fire. Jesus, she was going to burn me alive. Sweat beaded on my forehead, my skin and clothes damp, like I'd just been for a hard workout session. The heat went from uncomfortable to stinging. I bit my tongue. I didn't want to die screaming, not for this witch.

Banging came from upstairs. Was that the thundering of many feet? *Oh, please, merciful deities, be someone to save me.*

Snezana's brow furrowed, and she spun to face the doorway. The heat stopped. I took a deep breath of almost-relief. If that was just pizza delivery, I was still in trouble.

But there was a lot of rumbling, which could only mean multiple footsteps. "Down here!" I yelled. "Snezana's gone rogue. She's trying to burn me alive!"

"Shut it!" She kicked me in the stomach. I grunted. Dull pain radiated through my middle. "Wait here."

Well, I couldn't exactly go anywhere.

She made it up the first step then stopped, turned and raced back to me—quite a feat in those heels. She grabbed my straighter leg and dragged me along the concrete towards James. When we were halfway across, William, Beren, and four more uniformed PIB agents burst through the doorway, single file. They fanned out in a semi-circle, guns pointed at her, and blocked access to the door. Then her uncle entered, his face a thundercloud of anger.

Glory be to the PIB. I'd been saved! This time, my big breath out was all relief. I couldn't be happier, even to see William. Now, who'd have thunk it?

Snezana gasped. She dropped my leg and assumed a relaxed, just-hanging-out stance, as if that would make the scene look any better. "Uncle, what are you doing here?"

"I would ask you the same thing, Snezana." He looked past us to James's still body on the mattress. "Beren, attend to him, please."

"Yes, sir." Beren ran to James.

I called out to him. "She gave him a needle about ten minutes ago. I have no idea what was in it. Some kind of yellow liquid."

He held the needle up. "This one?"

"Yes."

He broke it open and smelled it, nodded, then put his hands on James.

"Why did you do it, Snezana? You know this is going to break your mother's heart."

"He promised to marry me, uncle, but that bitch, Millicent, refused to give him a divorce."

"That is such crap, obviously. Since when do you need to kidnap and drug someone who wants to be with you?"

She shot me a death glare. When she looked back at her uncle, she wore an angelic expression. "You know I don't like anyone saying no to me. You want me to be happy, don't you, uncle?"

Toot, toot, next train leaving for crazy town. All aboard.

He shook his head. "I love you like a daughter, Snezana, but this... I can't understand how...." He grabbed a handful of his own hair and pulled. This must be hard for him to accept. I also wondered if he was feeling the guilt of ignoring the signs that she was a few spells short of a grimoire.

For someone wearing heels, she had catlike reflexes. She bent and grabbed my ponytail, yanking my head back and pointing her finger at me. Every PIB gun followed her movement. *Yikes. Don't shoot.* I was so in the line of fire. My heart rate kicked up again. Sheesh, couldn't this just be over already? How was it the bad guys never knew when they were beat?

"What are you doing? You know they'll kill you if you kill me, right?"

"He's my uncle. He's the boss. There's no way he'll let them hurt a hair on my pretty head."

Oooookay. Tickets, please.

Drake took a step forward. "Please, Snezana. Just come with us quietly. You haven't killed anyone, so I can try and get you a lenient sentence. Don't make it worse."

A lenient sentence. I don't think so. Maybe he was just saying that to get her to play nice.

"Oh, but, uncle, it can't get any worse. If I can't have the man I love, then he can't have his sister." She wiggled her fingers, but before anything could happen, her uncle countered with his own finger wiggles, and her magic fizzled. *Phew!* Or maybe not.

Drake looked at me. His face paled. What? Was there a giant spider on my head? But then I felt it—my throat tightening. I tried to breathe in, but the airway had constricted. *Oh, shit!* I'd forgotten to renew my thought-protection spell.

"I'm so sorry, Lily. I'm a mind reader. Snezana! Retract the spell, this instant."

"Not unless you let me go and promise I can have him." She nodded towards James.

Air. I need air. Invisible fingers squeezed tighter and tighter. The crushing pain brought tears to my eyes. And God, I needed to breathe. It was hard not to panic, but the more I did, the less oxygen was in my system. Whenever we were dumped and dragged by a wave in the surf, we were told you had to go with it—relax until the churning was over, then it was safe to swim to the top. I pretended I was heading for the bottom, waiting for the time I could breathe again.

"Dammit, Snezana, stop it!" Her uncle sounded desperate.

"Nope." She had her arms crossed, and she was shaking her head, smiling. The fight inside me faded. I wasn't going to make it. My limbs felt like jelly. I gave in and tried to suck in a breath, but nothing was getting through. This was horrific, and only marginally better than dying by being burnt alive. I did my best to push down the rush of panic, but I was losing. I met William's gaze. His eyes were wide, pupils dilated, but then he grew calm and gave me a sweet smile. At least I'd die looking at his happy face. Blackness crept into my vision, and my eyes closed.

Bang! The part of my brain still paying attention registered a gunshot, although I'd never heard one in real life, but hey, I'd watched lots of cop shows. What was that going through my throat? Air! The pressure around my neck eased, and oxygen rushed in. I gulped great globs of it, taking it all in, loudly, greedily.

Someone helped me sit up, and the cuffs were removed. I opened my eyes. Snezana lay dead in front of me, her blood languidly spreading over the floor. Her uncle was on his knees, his hand on her chest, fingers sitting in her blood. His head hung low. Defeated, grieving. Sadness swelled in my chest, but not for her—I honestly couldn't give a crap that a psychopath was dead—but he was a man who had just lost someone he loved, and now he'd have to explain it to his sister. Coldness filtered through me, and I started shaking.

William crouched in front of me. He tilted my chin up so he could look into my eyes, probably to make sure I wasn't blue and about to die.

"Hi," I managed.

"Hi, yourself. Are you okay? Are you cold?" He took off his PIB jacket and put it around my shoulders. What a gentleman. He was always surprising me.

I snuggled into the jacket and tried to get warm. "Th— thanks. I'm k— kind of okay, and yes, f— freezing. But I'm alive, so that's something." My teeth were chattering but I forced a small smile. "Who shot her?"

His sad eyes said it all. "I'd do it again, too. Killing people is the worst part of the job, and we don't have to do it all that often, but I had no choice. She was killing you."

"Thanks, Will. I owe you one."

He smiled. "Nah, you found your brother and gave me my best friend back. We'll call this one even."

"Are you suggesting you're going to have to save my life again?"

"With you, anything's possible." I couldn't help but return his grin.

Beren approached us. "Hey, kids, there's someone over there who's dying to see you."

I cringed. "Bad word choice, mister." But my heart soared. I was finally going to see my brother awake and get a cuddle back, and before you remind me that I hate cuddles, this was a special circumstance.

William helped me up. I limped to the grimy mattress in the corner. James sat against the wall, dirty, mussed up, and looking like he'd been on a two-week bender, but his eyes were open, and his lips were curved into a smile. "Lily. You're the last person I expected to see."

"You know I like to do the unexpected." I dropped to my knees on the mattress and threw my arms around him. His trembling arms encircled me and squeezed. He reeked —no showers in a week would do that to a person—but I didn't care. I snuggled closer. "Don't ever run off with psychopathic kidnappers again. Millicent's been beside herself."

"What about you?" he rasped.

"You know me; I knew it would be fine."

"Such an optimist, sis."

"You know it." I pushed off the wall behind him and sat up to give him another once over. "You look like you've lost some weight. Did she feed you at all?"

"The first day she did, but she'd drugged it. How long have I been here?"

William spoke. "A week, dude. Sorry, we stuffed up. We never would've found you without your annoying sister's help."

"Hey, I'm not—"

"Just kidding." William playfully punched my arm. Where was this happy William before? Oh, that's right; he had his best friend back now. I was sure the joyful afterglow wouldn't last long. In fact, his serious face returned. "James, I know you've been unconscious for a while, but do you remember who took you? She had some help."

"Yes. It was payback. A couple of the guys from Eltham's gang. We put Eltham away about eight months ago. He's doing five years for drug trafficking. His cronies were only too happy to play along. Is she dead?" He tried to sit up and look over my shoulder, but he slumped back. Man, she'd really ruined him. I wanted to kill her, but luckily for her, she was already dead, because a shot to the heart was way nicer than what I had planned.

I looked around, and Snezana's uncle was busy talking to the other PIB agents on the other side of the room. I lowered my voice. "Yes, but she was ready to kill me, and she framed Millicent. Let's not even get into what she did to you, big bro. On one level, I'm sorry William had to kill her, but on another level, I'm not. What she did to you and me is going to stay with us forever." I would surely have the nightmares to prove it, and James probably would too. "Anyway, no more crime talk. Waddaya say, we get you home to your gorgeous wife?" His smile was weak, but it was there. Yep, it was all worth it. I was taking my brother home to the woman he loved. I was sure it would take a while for both of us to recover from what we'd been through, but there was no time like the present to start healing. "I hope you don't mind, but we'll just hop through Costa drive-through on the way."

My brother shook his head. "That's my sister."

I sure was.

CHAPTER 15

Taylor Swift pumped out of the speakers over the jubilant gathering. When I'd asked if I could hook my iPhone to her docking system, Angelica complied. She was quite on it for someone in their fifties. Canapé in hand, I chatted to Millicent and James, who had one arm slung around each other's backs. I didn't think they'd ever let go of each other again.

"Yeah, I have to book my flight back. I had to cancel one wedding already. I'd love to stay here forever, but it's time to go back to reality." Sigh—nothing lasted forever. I'd gotten the photos back to Tracy, but other work waited. I should be happy I'd had this much time with my brother.

James's forehead furrowed. "Lily, you should stay here, with us."

"I can't. My life's back in Australia… my job, my friends, my apartment."

"But you still have so much to learn about your magic, and Angelica can help you with that." It was true that I hadn't confirmed whether those ghostly images meant someone was going to die, and I was curious as to what else I was capable of. But was that enough to want to stay here, leaving Michelle and Sophie and the beach lifestyle I loved? "You can get work here, and why not rent your apartment out? And England's full of those historical buildings you love so much. You've already made new friends, and there's always Skype for your old ones." He had a point—goodness knew that was the only way we'd communicated for years. But moving countries was a crazy hassle, and who was to say they'd even grant me working status.

"I'd need visas, permission, stuff. Complicated stuff."

"Our mother was an English citizen, Lily. Just apply. You don't even need a visa. It'll be a piece of cake." *Mmm, cake.* Dessert was always my favourite part of a party, but it wasn't out yet. Damn.

I shook my head. "No, James. My adventure's over."

He whispered something in Millicent's ear. She nodded and made her way to another group of her friends. "Come with me." James grabbed my hand and led me to the back garden, where it was quieter. Fairy lights hung from the trees, whimsical and pretty. He sat us down on a concrete bench that had cherubs carved into the plinth-like legs.

"I've missed you, Lily, but that's not the only reason you should move here." He held out his hands and mumbled something. Four small, camel-coloured leather books popped into his upturned palms. He handed them to me.

"These were mum's diaries. I found them after she and Dad disappeared. I've read them a million times, and I think it's your turn to have them now. I'm glad I survived, because if I'd died, you never would've seen them. I haven't even told Millicent about them. There's something there. I kind of feel like they could help us find out what happened to Mum and Dad, but as many times as I've read them and been to some of the places they went to, I couldn't find a connection."

I drew in a quick breath. *He'd hidden these from me?* "But why wait until now to give them to me?" I stared at him, hoping he could see the hurt in my eyes. "You should've told me about these before. What the hell, James?"

He shook his head. "They had to be kept safe. Sorry, Lil." He bit his bottom lip. Argh, how could I be mad at him? I'd just gotten him back.

I put three of the diaries on my lap and turned the fourth over and over in my hands, enjoying the smooth feel of the leather. My mother had touched this, probably took it with her everywhere. I opened it. Most of the pages were filled. The last entry was dated the 29th July, 2008. The day she disappeared. I swallowed. I thought life had thrown everything at me, so I wasn't prepared for the bone-hollowing sadness that assaulted me. I clutched the book to my chest and sobbed. All those years she didn't get to hold her children, to live her life, to go on holidays, to laugh and cry with her family. James and I had been robbed, and it broke my heart every day—the only way to go on was to not think about it, but now I had access to her again in a way. If it wasn't rude to our guests, I'd run up to my room and read them all through without stopping.

James put a hand on my back and rubbed up and down. "I know. I miss them too." His breath hitched, and I knew he was trying not to cry. We'd both been through hell. Sometimes I was jealous that he was older and had more memories of them, but then that probably hurt him more. It scared me that I might forget things. There were already a couple of memories that were fraying at the edges, no matter how hard I tried to keep them together. Maybe these diaries would mend them.

"There's something else, Lily." Worry darkened his tone. "I never told you the full reason I decided to stay here."

"I figured Millicent was enough of a reason." I smiled through my tears then sniffled.

"She was, for sure, but I originally came over because Angelica paid a visit."

"What? You never told me. Why?"

"The day my powers came in, she appeared at uni when I was eating lunch outside." He laughed. "I thought she was nuts, of course, but she told me some things about Mum, stuff not just anyone could've known unless Mum had told them, and I made her prove her magic."

I giggled. "I did that too. As if I'd go off with just any old crazy who offered. I thought she was trying to kidnap me…" My voice sobered. "But it turned out you already had that covered."

"Yeah. I've decided I don't want another assistant. Maybe I'll share William's." He put his hand over mine on the diaries. "You're in danger, Lily. I've stayed here because I fit in so well, but also because working for the PIB gives me access to resources I wouldn't otherwise have. It's important we find out who's behind our parents' disappearance, Lily, because we're next. Someone's trying to end Mum's line."

I blinked, letting it sink in. Could this ride stop so I could get off? "But why?"

"I'm not sure. Angelica and I have a few theories. It might have something to do with the fact that we're the only living line with witches who can see the past and future. I don't have that skill, but I could pass it onto any children Millicent and I have, and they'll be in danger, just like you are. Angelica told me what happened, with those guys on the high street. They weren't working for Snezana. They're likely from the organisation trying to kill us."

Well, crap.

"William and Beren were there that day, because they know. They knew to keep an eye out for me, and when they found out you were in town, they had a word with Angelica, and she posted their detail to you."

"Oh, wow. I wondered how the police just happened to be in the right place at the right time. Have they been following me ever since?"

"Yep. And if they're not available, I have a few more friends willing to cover. You can't go back to Sydney. I don't have the resources to protect you there, and these diaries... you can't lose them. Find a safe place for them, and don't tell anyone. Mum didn't do anything without thought first. I think there're clues in there, Lily. All this started hundreds of years ago. I couldn't find anything to help unravel what's going on, but I think you might be able to. So, will you stay?"

His expectant gaze cut through me. It was just me and him. I could make a new home here, couldn't I? They had all the essentials, coffee, old buildings, and my brother, not necessarily in that order—*ahem*. I could pick up work here. Every community needed a photographer, right? I sucked in a deep breath, one of my favourite things to do since I'd had trouble the other day. "Okay. I'll stay."

His grin was brighter than all the fairy lights in all the gardens of the world. He jumped up. "Come with me." I struggled to hurry while juggling the diaries, which I slipped into a kitchen drawer before we went into the living room with the crowd.

James turned the music down. "Hey, everyone, can I have your attention?" The room stilled. "Lily said yes. My sister's staying in Westerham!" A cheer went up, and I blushed, new tears forming. Sheesh, I was such a cry-baby. Millicent ran in and gave me a hug. Angelica nodded, smiling. Beren wore his usual cute grin, and even William was beaming, except when my gaze met his, he toned it down. *Ha!* I saw you. I laughed.

"Well, if I knew you'd all be that welcoming, I'd have moved here years ago. Thank you."

"And there's one more thing." James turned to me. "I know we missed your birthday, but we didn't forget. Happy birthday to the best sister, sister-in-law, witch student, and criminal catcher ever."

The crowd shouted, "Happy birthday!" and cakes appeared out of nowhere, literally. Lots and lots of creamy, custardy, sugary goodness. William held a scrumptious-looking chocolate cake. James suddenly held a cake that was covered in cream and strawberries, Angelica held a fruit flan, and Millicent stepped forward with a black forest cake.

It seemed as if I'd already made friends here. Happiness expanded in my heart, pushing most of the sadness away. "Someone magic me a spoon; I've got some eating to do." Everyone cheered again. It didn't take much—these English were much more excitable than everyone gave them credit for, unless it was because of the alcohol. Yeah, it was probably just that.

Millicent handed me a spoon and plate with a piece of black forest cake. "Thanks, Mill." I licked my lips.

I smiled and thought back to that night, a month ago, when I'd felt abandoned and alone, wondering why my brother had forgotten me. Things sure could change quickly. I grinned and shovelled a massive piece of cake into my mouth. The worst birthday ever had just turned into the best.

Just like magic.

ALSO BY DIONNE LISTER

ABOUT THE AUTHOR

USA Today bestselling author, Dionne Lister is a Sydneysider with a degree in creative writing, two Siamese cats, and is a member of the Science Fiction and Fantasy Writers of America. Daydreaming has always been her passion, so writing was a natural progression from staring out the window in primary school, and being an author was a dream she held since childhood.

Unfortunately, writing was only a hobby while Dionne worked as a property valuer in Sydney, until her mid-thirties when she returned to study and completed her creative writing degree. Since then, she has indulged her passion for writing while raising two children with her husband. Her books have attracted praise from Apple iBooks and have reached #1 on Amazon and iBooks charts worldwide, frequently occupying top 100 lists in fantasy. She's excited to add cozy mystery to the list of genres she writes. Magic and danger are always a heady combination.

ACKNOWLEDGEMENTS

So many people to thank, as usual. This was my first foray into paranormal cosy mystery and first-person point of view, so it's been a tad scary but a gigantic ball pit of fun.

The very first thank you goes to the awesome woman who introduced me to Westerham: Andi. Thanks for showing me around and taking me for a yummy coffee at Costa. Can't wait to come back and do it again. Miss you all.

Thanks to my editor, Becky, at Hot Tree Editing, who lives in Australia but just happens to come from the UK. Her insight was invaluable.

To one of my bestest friends in the whole world, Jaime —a fellow author and word nerd. She proofread for me and asked some hard questions. I changed some stuff because of her, and it made my book better.

Thanks to Loukia, my gorgeous sister from another

mister (okay, and mrs), for answering a few questions—she lives near Westerham and was able to provide some awesome information. She even taught me how to say it properly: Westram. I'm not sure what happened to the other letters in there, but whatever.

Thanks to my hubby, who is almost as excited about this book as I am, which is a first, let me tell you.

To my cover guy, Robert Baird, I didn't know if you'd be able to change styles so easily, but you've outdone yourself again.

DEDICATION

To Ben, my son, because I promised, and I love you. Sorry you couldn't do the cover for this one, but maybe when you're a bit older.
And to MJ. Life keeps pushing you down, but you keep jumping back up with such class. You can teach us all a lesson in resilience and compassion. Love you, lady.